THE PENGUIN CLASSICS

FOUNDER EDITOR (1944–64) E. V. RIEU

Editor: Betty Radice

John Brough was born in 1917 and read Classics and Sanskrit at the universities of Edinburgh and Cambridge. He was Professor of Sanskrit at the University of London from 1948 to 1967 and then Professor of Sanskrit at the University of Cambridge and Fellow of St John's College. Although much of his research work has been devoted to textual studies in early Buddhist works and their Chinese translations, he has always maintained a serious concern for the purely literary aspects of Sanskrit.

POEMS
FROM THE SANSKRIT

*

TRANSLATED WITH AN
INTRODUCTION
BY
JOHN BROUGH

PENGUIN BOOKS

Penguin Books Ltd, Harmondsworth, Middlesex, England
Penguin Books, 625 Madison Avenue, New York, New York 10022, U.S.A.
Penguin Books Australia Ltd, Ringwood, Victoria, Australia
Penguin Books Canada Ltd, 2801 John Street, Markham, Ontario, Canada L3R 1B4
Penguin Books (N.Z.) Ltd, 182–190 Wairau Road, Auckland 10, New Zealand

—

This translation first published 1968
Reprinted 1969, 1977

—

—

Made and printed in Great Britain by
Cox & Wyman Ltd, London, Reading and Fakenham
Set in Monotype Bembo

Now to my Wife I dedicate my verse:
Some, She approved; and some, I trust, admired;
While this, She thought, was fair; and that, much Worse:
But, what is best in it, Herself inspired.

Contents

Introduction

THIS anthology of secular verses from classical Sanskrit represents an aspect of Sanskrit literature which is much less well known in the West than it deserves to be. It is probably true to say that, outside the small number of specialists, most Western readers have been scarcely aware of the existence of this highly civilized and artistic aspect of ancient Indian literature. On the other hand, the majority will undoubtedly have heard of the Upanishads and the Bhagavad-gītā, and many will have read at least something of these in one or other of the endless stream of translations. There can be small doubt that this disparity is due largely to the fact that, in contrast to some of the religious texts, the poetical literature has been rather badly served by translators. Relatively little has been readily available in English translation, and still less, unfortunately, in an English likely to persuade the reader that there is much literary value in the originals.

My hope is that the present volume – which is indeed only a small sample from the vast resources of Sanskrit poetry – may do a little towards redressing the balance, and may help to show English readers that Sanskrit literature does not consist exclusively of works like the Upanishads and the Bhagavad-gītā, and that life in ancient India was not universally passed in a haze of theosophical speculation and other-worldly religious preoccupations.

'Classical Sanskrit'

The language in which these verses were composed has often been called 'classical Sanskrit'; but the epithet 'classical' may be misleading. It is important to warn the reader that the situation is somewhat different from that of classical Latin or classical Greek. The choice of the term by earlier scholars is probably mainly due to the fact that Sanskrit holds a position, in relation to the modern languages of India, rather similar to that of Latin in respect of the modern languages of western Europe. Another factor seems to have been the purely grammatical observation that some analogies can be seen between the relationship of classical Attic Greek to Homeric Greek and that of 'classical Sanskrit' to the older language of the Vedas. In both cases, the older language shows a slightly more complex grammatical structure, and many differences in vocabulary. But the analogy is really somewhat superficial. The essential point which should be made clear is that, for centuries before the period with which we are concerned, the language of everyday life had already diverged so far from Sanskrit that the latter, throughout the whole period of what is called 'classical' literature, was purely a language of learning – in effect, a 'dead' language, as the term is usually understood, although it may perhaps seem perverse to label as 'dead' a language which continued so long in use as the living, flourishing vehicle of a vigorous and by no means moribund literature.

The position of 'classical Sanskrit' in relation to the civilization which produced it is thus in many ways less akin to that of classical Latin than it is to medieval Latin; and in some ways it would be not unreasonable to describe it as 'medieval Sanskrit', though here also the analogy must not be pressed too far. And it may well be felt that, in spirit, there are often affinities with the literature of post-classical Greek of the Hellenistic and Byzantine periods. There are in fact many verses in the Sanskrit anthologies which, in their content and style, would seem quite at home among the epigrams of the Greek Anthology.

Sources

The verses in this volume are my own selection; but they are for the most part drawn from existing Sanskrit anthologies compiled during the medieval period. The generic term in

Sanskrit for a verse of this type is *subhāṣita*, literally, 'that which is well said': in other words, a verse or poem which possesses literary merit, which can be justly included within the category of *belles lettres*. Many of these anthology verses were doubtless from the beginning individual, independent poems, the single stanza in Sanskrit being often of sufficient capacity to contain a poetic picture which, in Europe, would often have provided the substance of a lyric poem. Indeed, it has been said that, in the case of the longer and more elaborate metres, and because of the compactness and condensation of which Sanskrit is capable, a single four-line stanza may sometimes cover as much ground as many a European sonnet. It is only fair to add that some of these longer metres have in their four lines as many syllables as there are in eight or nine lines of an English pentameter. The verses which have come down to us under the names of Amaru and Bhartṛhari are presumably mostly independent poems of this type. In addition to these, however, a fair number of verses in the anthologies have been selected by the anthologists from longer works, in particular from the so-called 'court epics' (*mahā-kāvya*) and from the dramas. In some cases, the original work is still extant; and it is reasonable to suppose that many other anthology verses were also taken from such sources, the originals being no longer extant.

Although works in Sanskrit have continued to be composed until the present day, the great creative period of the literature lies between, approximately, the second century and the tenth century A.D. There are in fact very few extant works within our category which can with any confidence be dated earlier than about the fourth century; and the greater number of verses in the present collection are probably to be ascribed to the period fourth to tenth century. It is one of the misfortunes of Indian literature that, prior to the tenth century or thereabouts, very few literary works can be dated with certainty.

From the first millennium A.D., a number of collections of

verses have come down to us, most of which are ascribed to individual authors. Two of these, which bear the names of Bhartṛhari and Amaru respectively, have been drawn on for the present anthology. Of uncertain dates, both can nevertheless with some probability be attributed to about the fifth or sixth century, although earlier dates are not excluded by the evidence at present available. Both collections consist of separate, individual stanzas, each stanza in effect being an independent poem. For this reason they were naturally highly vulnerable to interpolation, and both have reached us in several different recensions, varying both in contents and in the order of verses, and it is certain that additional poems on the same themes were gradually incorporated. It has occasionally been suggested that these collections were from the beginning anthologies containing the verses of a number of poets. The arguments for this are perhaps slightly stronger in the case of Amaru, but nothing conclusive can as yet be decided. Making allowance for the later addition of verses, there does nevertheless seem to be in both cases a general impression of individuality, and there is at least a reasonable presumption that both Amaru and Bhartṛhari were themselves poets, and not merely anthologists. It is true that the matter would not be much advanced if this could be conclusively proved; for we have no information whatever about either except for the verses to which their names are attached. But this is a situation which they share with many other important names in Sanskrit literature.

From the later medieval period (eleventh century onwards) there have survived a number of collections which are quite explicitly anthologies of earlier poems. Three of the best known of these have contributed verses to the present volume: the *Subhāṣita-ratna-koṣa*[1] ('A Treasury of Fine Verses'), compiled

1. An English translation of the whole of this collection has been published by Professor D. H. H. Ingalls, under the title *An Anthology of Sanskrit Court Poetry*, Harvard Oriental Series, vol. 44, 1965.

by Vidyākara at the end of the eleventh century; the *Subhāṣitāvali* ('A Necklace of Fine Verses'), ascribed to Vallabhadeva, probably of the twelfth century, though with some later additions until the fifteenth century; and the *Paddhati* ('Manual' or perhaps better, simply 'Anthology') of Śārngadhara, of the fourteenth century. These are all very large collections, containing respectively 1,738, 3,527, and 4,620 verses. It may be remarked, however, that Śārngadhara has achieved his very large number by including in his Anthology a fair number of verses which no Indian critic would have considered to be poetry, but which were presumably valued by the compiler for the sake of the useful information they contained: for example, metrical spells against snake-bite; and instructions in verse for the preparation of a concoction for dyeing grey hair:

Take six parts of myrobalans, two parts
Of fibrous pomegranates, and three parts
Of turmeric, and pound them all together;
And then stir in six parts[1] of egg, and add
Of hair-oil twenty parts. Now place the whole
In iron vessel, covered with a lid
Also of iron. Bury in the ground,
Packed round with horse-dung. Leave it for a month.
Then mix with milk, until you have achieved
Ointment consistency. Massage it well
Into the scalp and beard. Wrap round with leaves
Of castor-oil plant, so that it will hold
In firm position while you sleep. Next day,
Rinse off when you awake. Three times repeat,
At seven-day intervals. And with this treatment
Your hair will stay, until your dying day,
As black and glossy as a bumble-bee.

1. The text, as printed in the edition, appears to say, 'the sixtieth part of an egg', which certainly seems an improbable quantity to try to measure. With no stronger reason than the intrinsic absurdity of such a niggardly amount of egg, I have risked an emendation of the sense.

I need hardly say that I have not included didactic verse of this type within the body of my own anthology. It would be too much to claim that all the verses which I have included are of the highest poetic merit; but still, for the most part they have been selected for at least some qualities of poetry in the originals, or some poetic charm of concept or felicity of expression. Here and there, it is true, I have admitted an occasional trifle of epigram, or frankly gnomic verse, especially if some touch of wit appeared to be present. And on a couple of occasions, even odd ethical verses, if they were bad enough to be (unintentionally) funny. But these are the exceptions.

Apart from the sources already mentioned, some verses have also been culled from a compilation made in modern times, *Indische Sprüche*, edited and translated into German by Otto Böhtlingk (3 volumes, 2nd edition, 1870–73). This enormous collection – 7,613 verses in all – has however not provided many verses for the present anthology, since it was compiled in the first place for purposes of lexicography rather than to illustrate literary merit. Apart from the Bhartṛhari and Amaru stanzas, which are incorporated in their alphabetic positions, and a handful of other exceptions, the greater number of the verses which it contains have little claim to rank as poetry. They are mostly sententious ethical or didactic verses, taken from the epics, books of fables and so forth, with an occasional more pointed epigram, but for the most part pedestrian and of little interest as literature.

In the medieval anthologies, the verses are arranged not according to author but by subject matter. Verses by the same poet are thus in many cases scattered widely in the anthology, although there is an occasional tendency to group together two or three of a poet's verses where they come within the same section. Many poets are named: in the *Subhāṣita-ratna-koṣa* some 220, in the *Subhāṣitāvali* about 350; but many verses are left without ascription. Where ascriptions can be checked, they are very often correct, but unfortunately enough of them are wrong to discourage us from placing too much reliance on those which are unsupported by other information. Sometimes, indeed, the same verse is attributed to different poets in different anthologies, and occasionally even in different manuscripts of the same anthology. In these circumstances, I have attached authors' names to the verses in the present volume only in the case of the better known poets, the others in any case being mostly mere names to us. Even these ascriptions, it should be added, are not all of equal certainty. The appearance of the name Amaru, for example, simply means that the verse in question occurs in one of the recensions of the Amaru collection, or, if it does not so occur, that it is attributed to Amaru by an anthologist. In some cases, naturally, more than one poet may share the same name. For example, it has been suggested that most of the verses attributed to Dharmakīrti are not by the great Buddhist logician of that name, but by another Dharmakīrti.

The classification of verses is along similar lines in the various anthologies, although details differ considerably. The *Subhāṣita-ratna-koṣa* opens with seven sections on various personages in the Buddhist and Hindu pantheons (a total of 150 verses), followed by Spring (39 verses), Summer (24 verses), the Rains (51 verses), Autumn (27), Early Winter (13), Late Winter (17), the God of Love (11), adolescence – with one exception, these verses are all concerned with the girl (50), the girl who has just reached maturity (81), on being in love (70), messages of the go-between (a woman friend or servant of the girl) (24), love-making (53), signs that love-making has taken place – this includes such signs as marks of biting and scratching (23), the woman angered – often for reasons of jealousy (65), the woman separated from her lover (52), and so forth.

The *Subhāṣitāvali* starts at stanza 581 a long series of verses on various animals, many of which are of course allegorical: Lions (41), Elephants (24), Deer (18), Peacocks (15), Geese (29),

Cuckoos (6), Bees (33), Cranes (7), Crows (13). Later, there are Trees (48), Clouds (21), the Ocean (39), Jewels (20), Lotuses (19). Later in the anthology we have: On Seeing the Girl (24), Praise of the Girl (7), her Hair (4), her Forehead (7), Eyebrows (3), Eyes (2), Ears (9), Nose (1), Lips (5), Face (16), Neck (4), Arms (2), Breasts (14), Waist (5), Body-hair (6), Buttocks (5), Thighs (5), Legs (3), Feet (3), her Anger (23), Reconciliation (20), Lovers' Dialogues (21), Spring (58), Summer (21), the Rains (75), and so on. Still later, we find Moonrise (52), followed three sections later by the Beginning of Love-making (44), Love-making (52), the conclusion of love-making (14), Descriptions of Dawn (71). In the whole anthology there are exactly 100 classified sections, while Śārngadhara has as many as 163 sections.

It may well be doubted whether any woman would be particularly pleased to have her charms listed in this determinedly systematic way; and I have not even attempted to emulate the Indian anthologists in this matter of taxonomy. In any case, a subject-matter classification is hardly workable in an anthology the size of the present volume; and since an arrangement by authors would be of little value when so many verses are anonymous or of doubtful authorship, I have made no attempt at all to arrange the translations according to either principle. The order of the verses is in effect haphazard, and such slight attention as has been given to arrangement has rather been directed towards diversification, partly in order that the reader, in reading consecutively, may thus be the more diverted, and partly to emphasize the very great diversity, not only of poetic value, but also of subject-matter and of styles, and the considerable richness of poetic invention and imagination shown by the poets. It is not to be imagined that all readers will like all the verses equally well; but the variety is such that I can reasonably hope that almost any reader will be able to find something here which will bring some pleasure and delight.

And this, after all, is by no means the least of the justifications for the existence of poetry.

> Poets today too often try to preach,
> Or private feelings show to public view:
> These antique verses do not seek to teach,
> But simply poetry's pleasures to renew.

Since many of the verses are, as already remarked, taken from longer works, I have included in the anthology a small sample of the two main types of these works, namely, the drama, and the cultivated epic poem, both examples being taken from the works of the outstanding poet Kālidāsa.

The general problem of translation

So much has already been written by others on the theory of translation that I am reluctant to add still more words to the debate, and am aware that I have no profound originalities to contribute to the theory. Since, however, the reader of a translated poem may reasonably expect some information about the relationship of the translation to the original, some remarks on the practice of the craft, with some illustrative examples, may not come amiss.

We need not spend much time on the old controversy of prose against verse. Obviously, good prose is better than bad poetry, and even a plain prose rendering is probably preferable to a vapid version in verse. In the latter case, the reader judges the lack of merit in the English verse, and instinctively concludes that the original must be of the same standard of mediocrity. But in the case of a prose translation, the basis of judgement is different, since there only the sense-content of the original, and not a poetical form, is presented as evidence. Probably the best examples of effective translations into prose are to be seen in the case of longer narrative poems, such as epics: understandably, since there the flow of the narrative sense, while it may not be the sole factor enjoyed by a reader of the original, is none the less sufficiently dominant to sustain the work. At the same time, it is also easy to designate other prose translations where insensitive, insipid language has been most successful in bleaching out all qualities of charm and beauty, in virtue of which the originals may have the right to rank as authentic poetry. Indeed, so many of the English translations of Sanskrit which I have seen are bleached and wrung out in this way that it is difficult to avoid the conclusion that the translators have been sworn enemies of Sanskrit literature.

For reasons which are not obvious to me, it has in recent years become fashionable to decry the critical acumen of my old teacher, Arthur Berriedale Keith, and inconsiderately disparaging remarks have been made on this score, not only by those who had no right to speak at all, either as scholars or as critics, but even by one or two scholars whose scholarship I respect, even if, as it would seem, they have not taken the trouble to remember what Keith had written. It is for this reason, and not only for reasons of *pietas*, that I quote at rather greater length than otherwise would have been necessary. Professor Ingalls goes as far as to say, 'It is obvious from his works that for the most part he disliked Sanskrit literature. There are only two classical authors to whom he allows full praise, Kālidāsa and Bhavabhūti.'[1] Keith, however, wrote as follows in the Preface to his History of Sanskrit Literature:

'The neglect of Sanskrit Kāvya is doubtless natural. The great poets of India wrote for audiences of experts; they were masters of the learning of their day, long trained in the use of language, and they aim to please by subtlety, not simplicity of effect. They had at their disposal a singularly beautiful speech, and they commanded elaborate and most effective metres. Under these circumstances it was inevitable that their works should be difficult, but of those who on that score pass them by it may fairly be said *ardua dum metuunt amittunt vera viai*. It is in the great writers of Kāvya alone, headed by Kālidāsa, that we

1. op. cit., p. 50.

find depth of feeling for life and nature matched with perfection of expression and rhythm. The Kāvya literature includes some of the great poetry of the world, but it can never expect to attain wide popularity in the West, for it is essentially untranslatable; German poets like Rückert can, indeed, base excellent work on Sanskrit originals, but the effects produced are achieved by wholly different means, while English efforts at verse translations fall invariably below a tolerable mediocrity, their diffuse tepidity contrasting painfully with the brilliant condensation of style, the elegance of metre, and the close adaptation of sound to sense of the originals. I have, therefore, illustrated the merits of the poets by Sanskrit extracts, adding merely a literal English version.'

I have re-read this paragraph with close attention, but I have not been able to discover any hidden meaning in it; and I do not understand how such words could be written by one who 'for the most part disliked Sanskrit literature'. I am nevertheless led to wonder whether a memory of these remarks of Keith had anything to do with the decision of some subsequent translators to eschew poetry, and to favour prosaic English as their chosen medium for the translation of Sanskrit poems.

For my part, I have been more rash, and have risked using English verse-forms, being persuaded that the English reader might otherwise remain unconvinced that this was anything even faintly related to poetry. I am well aware that there is a risk; and it is not entirely satisfactory to shelter behind the thought that, if a verse is judged successful, the translator may arrogate to himself some credit, while if it fails, the fault can be fobbed off on the original poet. Better, perhaps, to invoke the defence supplied by Chaucer:

> 'This may wel be rym dogerel,' quod he.
> 'Why so?' quod I, 'why wiltow lette me
> Moore of my tale than another man,
> Syn that it is the beste rym I can?'

And there is, after all, no law of nature to compel a translator to be tepid and diffuse, although it must be admitted that Keith's strictures are all too often applicable. On the other hand, it is a little unfair to object that effects in a wholly different language are achieved by wholly different means, since this is of the nature of translation. The use of a different language in itself involves the use of wholly different means, and here it is indeed a fact of nature that languages do differ very widely in grammatical structure and in the whole apparatus of vocabulary. If Sappho's

> φαίνεταί μοι κῆνος ἴσος θέοισιν
> ἔμμεν

can be magically rendered into Latin, with metre identical, grammatical structure the same, and one word corresponding to one word,

> ille mi par esse deo uidetur,

this required not only the genius of Catullus, but also the happy accident of a close similarity between the two grammars; and not even Catullus could keep it up throughout the whole poem. Where the languages are as far apart as Sanskrit and English, we can never hope for a word-grammar-metre correspondence of this type.

Whether we like or not, whether we translate a poem into prose or into verse, we cannot possibly give the reader the same poem as the original. A literal prose version may often give more of what can be called the sense-content, but often at the cost of concealing something which may be equally important, namely, the fact that the original is a poem. To take an extreme illustration:

> pāṇau padmadhiyā madhūkamukulabhrāntyā tathā gaṇḍayor
> nīlendīvaraśankayā nayanayor bandhūkabuddhyādhare . . .

Not great poetry, admittedly; but still poetry, and quite gracefully expressed. Yet, let us translate with the most precise identification of the flowers mentioned:

'(The bees think that) your hands are *Nelumbo nucifera*, that your cheeks are buds of *Bassia latifolia*, that your eyes are blossoms of *Nymphaea stellata* var. *cyanea*, that your lips are *Pentapetes phoenicea* (or *Terminalia tomentosa*)',

and how shall we convince the English reader that there is any poetry here at all?

Now, Sanskrit verses are shapely. They have a very definite and strict metrical form, and often have extremely complex and subtle sound patterns of assonance and alliteration. The qualities of rhythm, of shapeliness, of the music of the words, cannot be directly transferred to another language, and there is no perfect solution. We seek, in fact, the best approximate solution which our limitations will allow; and these limitations, it must be remembered, are not only the limitations of our own abilities imposed by nature, but also include those imposed by the nature of the receiving language. The attempt often involves what seems to the translator to be a complete dismemberment of the original verse into constituents of sense, and the subsequent creation of a new poem, where these constituents are rebuilt and constrained, often with much labour, into a new formal pattern of words. The most that can be hoped for is that, in the more successful examples, the new poem, while carrying as much as possible of the sense-content of the original, will also convey to the reader some atmosphere similar to that of the original poem. Naturally, this is not always achieved.

There are usually many possibilities in the receiving language and the task of the translator may often seem to be mainly the discarding of the less satisfactory alternatives, and the attempt to find a better one. And in this he may often be pulled in two directions, when one alternative makes for a better equivalent to the poetic value of the original, while the other is more faithful to the sense-content, but is poetically inferior.

The almost boundless possibilities, and the extent to which a translation may in part reflect, in part distort a poem, can best be illustrated by translation from English into English. Try to forget the original, and consider the following as a plain prose rendering of a *Hymn to Diana*:

Royal goddess of the hunt, beautiful maiden, the sun is now sleeping. Take your place on your throne of silver, ruling with the dignity you always possess. The evening star comes as a suppliant to beg for your light, most brilliant of goddesses.

There may be nothing terribly offensive in such a version, and the reader may even be able to feel, though but dimly, that the original had some poetic merit; but the thought-content is undeniably slight, and it may be difficult to convince him that the original was worth the bother of translating. We can then, without too much difficulty, produce an alternative version in rhyme and metre:

Fair maiden, huntress, goddess chaste, and queen,
The sun has set. Come, mount your silver throne,
And let your ever-gracious light serene
To us and to the evening-star be shown.

There is no great offence here either, and probably enough of the sense of the original remains to allow us to pass the verse as a reasonably fair translation, as translations go; yet neither is there any merit, and the flatness of the verse may conceal the original poetry even more effectively than the prose. And yet the reader who must rely on translations to learn something of a foreign poetry may consider himself fortunate if he is presented with nothing worse than this: for with approximately equal philological justification, and only a little more padding, I might have given him:

O maiden goddess of the silvery moon,
The sun doth slumber. Grant us then thy boon,
Enthroned in state, as always heretofore:

For Hesperus doth join us to implore,
Bright lady, huntress of the enchanted night,
The blessing of thy ever-brilliant light.

And if you dismiss this as worthless, it will not help in the least if I protest that the original verse is considered by many to be a lyric of great merit within its own literature: for this will only invite you to conclude that the rest of the literature must be dreadful indeed. And so we could continue to produce all sorts of varying paraphrases in verse, some worse, some better; but it is unlikely that even the best among them would convey to the reader the poetical qualities of what Ben Jonson actually wrote:

Queen and Huntress, chaste and fair,
  Now the sun is laid to sleep,
Seated in thy silver chair
  State in wonted manner keep:
    Hesperus entreats thy light,
    Goddess excellently bright.

The translator is constantly discouraged by this multiplicity of possible renderings; and in the end, all he can do is to hold fast to the faith that, if he exerts himself to use 'the beste rym he can', the resulting verse may give to the reader at least some of the qualities of the original.

It is self-evident that the better the original poetry is, the more difficult is the translator's task. But certainly in the more light-hearted verses, or satirical epigrams, a verse-rendering may often seem to be preferable to literal prose, even at the expense of some slight adjustments in the literal sense. For example:

In Hamburg lebten zwei Ameisen,
Die wollten nach Australien reisen.
Bei Altona auf der Chaussee
Da taten ihnen die Beine weh,
Und da verzichteten sie weise
Dann auf den letzten Teil der Reise.

In Hamburg there lived two ants who made up their minds to travel to Australia. Then, on the pavement at Altona (just outside Hamburg) their feet hurt; and thereupon they sensibly gave up the last part of the journey.

But the English reader may perhaps get more of the bite of the original epigram from:

Two ants who lived in London planned
To walk to Melbourne overland.
But, footsore in Southampton Row,
When there were still some miles to go,
They thought it wise not to extend
The journey to the bitter end.

Or, from the Greek Anthology,

ἐντὸς ἐμῆς κραδίης τὴν εὔλαλον Ἡλιοδώραν
ψυχὴν τῆς ψυχῆς αὐτὸς ἔπλασσεν Ἔρως.

Eros himself has fashioned (as a sculptor) within my heart the sweet-voiced Heliodora, the soul of my soul.

The god of love has carved with sculptor's art
My soul's sweet-talking soul within my heart.

Or,

ἡ τὰ ῥόδα, ῥοδόεσσαν ἔχεις χάριν· ἀλλὰ τί πωλεῖς;
σαυτήν, ἢ τὰ ῥόδα, ἠὲ συναμφότερα;

Rose-girl, pretty as roses,
What is it you sell?
Yourself? Or just the roses?
Or rose and girl as well?

As Keith remarked, verse-translations are too often tepid and diffuse. One of the main reasons for this is the remarkable ease with which so many translators succumb to the temptation to add padding. One of the most reckless examples of this which I have encountered is the well known version by William Johnson Cory of Callimachus's lines on the death of Heraclitus, also from the Greek Anthology. Making allowance for reasonable substitutions, such as 'are awake' for 'live', or 'Carian' for 'of Halicarnassus', I have enclosed within brackets the words which have no justification at all:

They told me, Heraclitus, (they told me) you were dead,
They brought me (bitter news to hear and bitter) tears (to shed).
(I wept as) I remembered how often you and I
Had tired the sun (with talking and sent him down the sky).
And now that thou art (lying), my (dear old) Carian guest,
(A handful of grey) ashes, (long,) long ago (at rest),
(Still) are thy (pleasant voices, thy) nightingales, awake;
For Death, (he) taketh all away, but these he cannot take.

The Greek original has none of this sugary sentimentality, but a simplicity and dignity which Mr Cory has destroyed utterly:

εἶπέ τις, Ἡράκλειτε, τεὸν μόρον, ἐς δέ με δάκρυ
ἤγαγεν, ἐμνήσθην δ' ὁσσάκις ἀμφότεροι
ἥλιον ἐν λέσχῃ κατεδύσαμεν· ἀλλὰ σὺ μέν που,
ξεῖν' Ἁλικαρνησεῦ, τετράπαλαι σποδιή,
αἱ δὲ τεαὶ ζώουσιν ἀηδόνες ᾗσιν ὁ πάντων
ἁρπακτὴρ Ἀίδης οὐκ ἐπὶ χεῖρα βαλεῖ.

They told me of your death, and brought me tears:
For I recalled the many times we sent
The sun to bed. But, though the time will come
When you are ancient dust, in distant years,
Your nightingales will live; and Death, intent
To pillage all things, cannot make them dumb.

Of course, if any readers actually prefer the nineteenth-century version, I will not quarrel about literary taste; but I can assure them that the second version is very much nearer to the Greek.

Admittedly, it must be accepted that padding is not always as harmful as Cory's. Thus:

πέμπω σοι μύρον ἡδύ, μύρῳ παρέχων χάριν, οὐ σοί·
αὐτὴ γὰρ μυρίσαι καὶ τὸ μύρον δύνασαι

I send you perfúme, for the perfume's sake,
Not yours: you can perfume the perfume's scent,

which Jonson expanded into:

I sent thee late a rosy wreath,
Not so much honouring thee
As giving it a hope that there
It could not wither'd be;
But thou thereon didst only breathe
And sent'st it back to me;
Since when it grows, and smells, I swear,
Not of itself but thee.

The Greek here is a pretty trifle, upon which Jonson has based a poem of beauty, which deserves its place in the canon of English lyric. (But to appreciate the excellence of the poetry, it is essential to read it as poetry, and to delete from the memory the wretched Colonel's miserable tune.) With such encouragement I have not felt it necessary to exclude absolutely from the present anthology an occasional verse which had gathered a modicum of padding, if the verse as a whole seemed reasonably faithful to the intention of the original. But such verses are very few, and among them, I think there is only one where the quantity of padding is comparable to Jonson's, and none as bad as Cory's. By way of atonement, there is one instance where a Sanskrit verse of seventy-six syllables has been reduced to thirty syllables in the translation, though I think the message of the epigram in this case remains essentially unaltered.

While it is usually possible to avoid padding, some degree of reworking or paraphrasing is often inevitable; and sometimes also a rearrangement of the order of ideas can also be very helpful towards the construction of the new formal pattern, especially when a strict scheme of rhyme and metre is involved. Naturally, such rearrangement must be avoided if the order is an important aspect of the original verse. But in many cases it is relatively harmless. For example, in Villon's *Ballade des menus propos*:

Je congnois bien mouches en let,
Je congnois a la robe l'omme,
Je congnois le beau temps du let,
Je congnois au pommier la pomme,
Je congnois l'arbre a veoir la gomme,
Je congnois quant tout est de mesmes,
Je congnois qui besongne ou chomme,
Je congnois tout, fors que moy mesmes.

A ballade is an excellent five-finger exercise for a translator; but to make it easier for myself, I have allowed a ten-syllable line for the eight of the original. First, line 1: 'I know well flies in milk'. We need five further lines to rhyme with line 1, and it is therefore unprofitable to try to shape a metrical line ending in 'milk'. Line 3: 'I know good weather from bad.' For this, we might try:

I know when days are hot, and when they're cool.

This may be more promising, and can rhyme with the first line of the third stanza:

Je congnois cheval et mulet:

I know which is the horse and which the mule.

Then, in stanza 2, line 6, we observe:

Je congnois fols nourris de cresmes.

This will serve very well, if we bring it up to the position of line 3 in its stanza:

I know that cream not seldom feeds a fool.

Returning to stanza 1, 'pool' suggests itself for the rhyme. In the end, after some trial and error, and with similar regard for the interlocking rhymes in the other stanzas, we can arrive at a version where the lines of the original are rearranged in the order 1, 4, 3, 6, 5, 2, 7, 8:

I know that flies make milk their swimming-pool,
I know the apple from the apple-tree,
I know when days are hot, and when they're cool,
I know when it is best to let things be,
I know where I'll find amber presently,
I know on sight a sloven or a beau,
I know which is the drone and which the bee,
I know all else, myself I'll never know.

This is of course an extreme example, where each line is a separate sense-unit, and where the order of these units within each stanza is not unduly important. Usually, it is not feasible to rely so heavily on rearrangement.

Some of the special problems

Sanskrit is a highly inflected language, with a grammatical structure of a type similar to Latin and Greek, though slightly more complicated than either. In addition, it developed in the classical period a quite remarkable capacity for building very long nominal compounds, which are frequently used in poetry, and often very effectively. For example, in verse no. 222 the cat is described by the adjectives *ā-kubjī-kṛta-pṛṣṭham*, 'having-a-somewhat-made-into-a-hump-back', and *unnata-valad-vakrāgra-puccham,*[1] 'having-a-raised-twisting-crooked-tip-tail', while the dog rejoices in the epithet *lālākīrṇa-vidīrṇa-sṛkka-vikacad-daṃṣṭrā-karālānanaḥ*, 'having-a-saliva-smeared-split-open-

1. The text as printed in the Harvard edition has *vaktra* 'face', which does not make satisfactory sense in the context, and which should be emended to *vakra* 'crooked' for which it is a simple scribal error.

mouth-corners-expanding-teeth-fearsomely-gaping-face'. This gives to the verbal expression of the original a sense of energy and urgency which obviously cannot be imitated by any comparable formal means in a language like English. Clearly, the use of such compounds, as well as the generally tightly knit, concise inflexional structure of the language, can endow the verses with structural qualities which are often very important to the poetry. But all that can be done in translation is to attempt to recreate by quite different means, in some measure, the emotional impact of the original; and we are more likely to achieve an approximation to this if we use the linguistic resources which English provides, rather than strain to imitate structural features of the original which English cannot accommodate. The artificial use in English of long compounds, for example, would usually destroy more important poetical qualities of the original, and would convey to the reader an impression quite different from that received by the original audience.

Another feature of Sanskrit poetry which cannot be adequately matched in a translation is the great wealth of synonyms or near-synonyms which the poet had at his disposal. It has often been said – or so I am told – that English has an exceptionally rich vocabulary. Indeed, I am in no position to assess the justice of this claim in any general terms, though I have no doubt that most of us who use English find its vocabulary more or less adequate for most prosaic purposes. But, for the purposes of poetry, English, in comparison with Sanskrit, is poor in the extreme. There is very little a translator can do about this; but in fairness the reader should be told. Where, for example, Sanskrit may have some fifty expressions for 'lotus', the English translator has only 'lotus', and he must make the best of it. It is true, as others have remarked, that the Sanskrit poet is influenced frequently in his choice among the many available synonyms by considerations of metre; and it is true that in theory it would usually be possible to find a word for 'lotus' to fit almost any metrical position in the verse (at least from two to five syllables). But it would be a mistake to imagine that this made the technical task of the poet easy. It is hard to say to what extent the ready interchange of synonyms encouraged the development of the extremely complex and difficult classical metres, and to what extent the strict metrical patterns forced the poets to extend their range of synonyms. But anyone who believed that Sanskrit poetry could be written merely by using a good synonym-dictionary would soon be disenchanted. Nothing so quickly discriminates a good poet from a mediocre one as does the ease and flow of the music of the verse. Verses which are actually faulty in metre are virtually unknown in the classical period – mistakes in metre would at once condemn a poet to oblivion: but even so, among metrically correct verses there are vast differences. The choice among synonyms, for a good poet, is not merely a matter of metre, but also, and much more, a question of euphony and the harmonious structure of the verse as a whole. And for the translator, the sore point is that the ringing of the changes among the Sanskrit synonyms imparts a richness to the texture of the poetry which cannot be matched in English. Nor is there any remedy in seeking to translate 'literally', giving 'water-born' for *ambujam* and *vāri-jam*, or 'mud-born' for *pankajam*: since on the one hand such expressions, though etymologically accurate, are fantastic in English, while the Sanskrit words are normal; and on the other hand, the Sanskrit words do in fact *mean* 'lotus', and nothing else. It is worth remarking that not every possible synonym for the individual parts of these compounds can be employed in this sense. Thus, *uda-ja*, equally meaning 'water-born', does not appear to mean 'lotus', though it may be applied to fish or water-weeds, whereas *ambu-ja* could hardly be used of fish; and *udaka-ja* does not seem to occur at all, and would probably not be used of lotuses, although *udaka* is as common a word for 'water' as *ambu* or *vāri*.[1] As against this, it is possible (though I hesitate to be dogmatic) that any permutation of synonyms in the two parts of the compound 'earth-supporter' will always result in the meanings 'king' and 'mountain'. Naturally, this compound-matrix was readily used for double senses involving kings and mountains.

It would perhaps be hardly fair to say that all the multifarious terms applied to the lady in the love-poems are in fact synonymous; but for the practical translator, who may feel that in the poem one complimentary expression may be as good as another, they often present much the same situation as the lotus. Here again, it is quite impossible to attempt literal translations in most cases. We cannot, while retaining our gravity, address the lady in a serious love-poem as 'O slender-waisted one', or 'O thou of the thin limbs', or 'O thou of the (horizontally) wide eyes', or 'Thou with long external corners to the eyes', or 'Lady with fine buttocks', or 'Girl with well-rounded hips', or other similar terms of endearment, well-intended though they undoubtedly are. In some places the translator can replace such expressions with something not too dissimilar from the rather limited range which English poetry can readily accept; and in other cases it is simpler, and more effective, to substitute the simple pronoun: 'You', or 'She'. From the point of view of literalness, this may at first sight seem to be obviously unfaithful to the Sanskrit original; but in many cases it may well be that in this way the effect of the verse as a whole is in the end more faithful to the intention of the Sanskrit poet.

A frequent feature of Sanskrit literary works, both in verse and in ornate prose, is the employment of words and phrases with double meanings, and the language has a quite unparalleled capacity for punning on an extensive scale. This was developed to such an extent that in the later period whole epics were

1. It is true that *udaka* is usually (though not universally) avoided in poetry, as being too 'prosaic' a word.

composed which could be read in two or even more senses. Thus, it was possible to write a single set of words, from which can be understood either the story of the *Rāmāyaṇa* or that of the *Mahā-bhārata*, according to how the words of the individual verses are interpreted. On epic scale, this can become a little tedious, although the extraordinary skill and ingenuity of the authors must surely command our admiration, even if we must admit that such creations can seldom rise to the heights of poetry. The intellectual achievement may reasonably be considered as at least as admirable as the skill of a grand master at chess. But it would be a mistake to imagine that the use of punning is in itself necessarily fatal to poetry; and on a smaller scale, double senses are frequently employed by poets most effectively. In contrast to English, where puns are usually humorously intended, Sanskrit authors can use them quite seriously, although they are admittedly often employed quite light-heartedly, as an added embellishment of the verse. When Bhartṛhari, for example (ed. Kosambi, 139), sets forth the charms of the young girl in terms where each item can be alternatively interpreted in a religious sense, this is merely to lead up to the climax of the verse, expressed as an apparent paradox. It would be quite absurd here to imagine that this verse, which is merely a graceful *jeu d'esprit*, was in any way an expression of a divided mind, wavering between love and religion.

Only on the rarest of occasions a lucky chance of language may make it possible to reflect a pun in the receiving language; and usually, verbal play, if it is essential to the verse, makes the verse in question untranslatable. To take a rather trivial example (Bhartṛhari, 131):

> mukhena candrakāntena mahānīlaiḥ śiroruhaiḥ
> pāṇibhyāṃ padmarāgābhyāṃ reje ratnamayīva sā.

'Since her face had the beauty of the moon, and her hair was jet-black, and her hands were the colour of lotuses, she seemed to be all made of jewels.' Nothing can be done to make this into an acceptable verse in another language, since it does not even make sense until the reader knows that *candrakānta*, in addition to meaning 'having the beauty of the moon', is also the name of a precious stone; that *mahānīla* means 'very black' and also 'sapphire'; and that *padmarāga* means 'lotus-coloured' and also 'ruby'.

In most cases, therefore, verses with double meanings have had to be omitted from the present anthology. A few, however, have been admitted, if the double sense did not penetrate the verse as a whole, or if it could be to some extent adapted (usually, of course, in rather attenuated form), or where the neglect of one of the meanings still left a reasonably acceptable verse in English. By way of compensation, I have on a couple of occasions allowed a punning sense in verses where the originals have no comparable puns – merely because this type of thing is so typical of Sanskrit, and deserved to be illustrated somewhere in the anthology. The reader may safely be left to identify these examples for himself.

Poetical conventions and attitudes

Difficulties can often arise from content as well as from form. Sometimes, with a little care, the translator may be able to do something to resolve such difficulties, or may be able to deal with them in such a way as to present less of a stumbling-block to the reader. Still, it would be unfair to attempt to eliminate or disguise characteristic conventions or poetic conceits merely because they are unfamiliar to western readers. Among such conceits, which were taken for granted by the Sanskrit poets and their audience, we may cite the fancies that the Ashóka-tree comes into full blossom only after it has been kicked by a beautiful girl, with jangling anklets; that, similarly, the Bakula requires a similar maiden to sprinkle its roots with wine from her mouth; and that the Champaka awaits the vision of her wine-flushed moon-face. With regard to conceits of this type, the translator may reasonably plead for clemency. At the worst, such things may be considered as artificialities, tedious if used too frequently, but on the whole fairly harmless in themselves.

In any case, it would hardly be fair to pass adverse judgement on a literature because of attitudes and conventions which were not in any sense faults from the point of view of the original authors and audiences. We may be tempted to say that any literature, however exotic to our own, must be read and assessed with full acceptance of its own conventions. This, however, is not quite the end of the matter for the translator. As readers of foreign literatures, we are bound to such acceptance, on penalty of completely missing the point, and of being hampered in appreciation by irrelevant considerations. But, if we are translating into English, we are also attempting to produce an English poem, and must therefore pay some heed to what is and what is not acceptable in English. Naturally, there is no law against the incorporation of exotic concepts and attitudes, and there is no definite point at which these can be said to cease intrinsically to be acceptable. But sometimes there is indeed a limit, and if we transgress it, we risk bathos at the least. If the risk seemed too great, I have not attempted to include the verse in question among the translations. For example, the walk of a young woman is sometimes compared with that of an elephant; and even the western reader, if he has seen the grace and majesty of the elephant's slow gait, might admit that the comparison is by no means derogatory to the lady. But I confess that it is difficult to use such a comparison in an English verse without the result seeming to be comic or worse. A similar comparison with the goose is less difficult, provided we remember that the poets had in mind not the ungainly farmyard bird but the wild goose. The effect of this comparison has often been spoiled by European translators, many of whom have substituted the swan for the goose, presumably because they felt that swans are more 'poetical'. But there are no swans in Sanskrit literature, and I have not hesitated to admit geese into the translations.

When archaeologists have shown that woman's use of paint and powder has been constant since the dawn of civilization, it may on reflection seem surprising that references to this feminine characteristic are somewhat rare in European poetry. In fact, when the matter is mentioned at all, it is usually in terms of disparagement, as in John Donne's epigram:

> Thy flattering picture, *Phryne*, is like thee,
> Onely in this, that you both painted be;

or, by Pope, in gentler satire in *The Rape of the Lock*, 'Puffs, powders, patches . . .' In India, it must be admitted, religious writers, especially Jains and Buddhists, were often savage on the subject of women. But the cultivated, civilized Sanskrit poets for the most part saw nothing reprehensible in woman's predilection for adornment of jewel or paint. On the contrary, cosmetics as well as jewellery are freely admitted into poetry, as an entirely natural aspect of feminine behaviour, as a trait which, far from evoking criticism, was clearly felt to be rather endearing. In addition to the painting of the face, the reader should take note of the application of cosmetics to the breasts, and the regular use of red lac on the soles of the feet.

A feature of this poetry which western readers may at first find tedious is the constant recurrence of stock comparisons: the lady's face is like the moon, her eyes like lotuses, to mention only two of the more frequent. At the same time, it should be observed that the better poets hardly ever use this inherited stock-in-trade, whether the Ashóka flowering after being kicked, or the moon and the girl's face, without imparting some touch of their own. It was considered to be no small part of the merit of a good poet to be able to take such run-of-the-mill materials, and, by the exercise of an unusual perceptive faculty, to transform them into something new, in exactly the same manner in which he would transmute a familiar feature of the world or of human society, by means of the insight which Ānandavardhana, writing on the theory of poetry in the ninth century A.D., called 'that strange vision of poets which is always new'. As has been said:

The poet's purpose is not just to say
  The moon is like the lady's face,
But to express it in a different way,
  And with a certain grace.

And indeed, grace and elegance of expression, coupled with poetic perceptiveness, are important characteristics of Sanskrit poetry.

In addition to some exotic poetic conceits, the reader must be prepared to meet with certain other things which are not necessarily familiar to him, at least in literature: for example, love-making, as described in considerable detail by Sanskrit poets, is often passionate in specific ways which, it may be presumed, are not rare in actuality in Europe, but which European poets have usually hesitated to express with any frankness in their verses. Indeed, there are some aspects of love-making, quite frequent in Sanskrit poetry, of which, I suspect, it would be difficult to find even a hint among the love-poems of Europe. Apart from these, it may be remarked that biting is frequent: next day, the girl's standard excuse is that she has been stung on the lip by a bee. So also is scratching: and the girl may either with some pride display to her friends the weals on her breasts and elsewhere, as proof that she really has been loved; or, if she is by nature more modest, she may attempt the excuse (though with little chance of being believed) that she has been scratched by the thorn-bushes in the garden.

From representations in art, many readers will already be

familiar with the classic ideal of Indian feminine beauty: breasts so well developed that not even a thread of a lotus-filament could find space between them; or, from the other point of view, scarcely able to find room between her two arms: so that her exceedingly slender wasp-waist is constantly taxed with the effort of supporting the burden; while below, her heavy hips largely contribute to her swaying gait, and make the business of walking a tiring process.

The fact that the lotus closes its blossoms at sunset (though there are also 'night-lotuses' which close during the day), and such other details of the exotic background as occur in the verses in this volume, can mostly be readily deduced from context, and need not be writ large here. It will be observed also that while spring, as in the west, is certainly a season appropriate to the awakening of love, the coming of the monsoon rains, with their thunder-clouds and the dancing and the screaming of the peacocks, has for the poets an even greater significance in this respect. Of the few points of the mythological background which are relevant, we may mention the fact that the gods churned the primeval ocean in order to obtain the nectar of immortality; that the god of love has five flower-arrows, that his bow is strung with bees, whose buzzing represents the twang of the bow-string; and that he was burnt to ashes by the fire from the eye of the god Shiva. On this last point, see also the introductory note to the selection from the *Kumārasambhava*, on page 107.

It is no doubt natural that the medieval anthologies should devote a very large proportion of their space to verses on the theme of love. Such verses have sometimes been called 'love-poems' or 'love-lyrics'; and there is no great harm in such designations, provided it is made clear that they are not love-poems in the sense that the term is often used in the West. In the case of Sappho and Catullus, and countless other Europeans, the poem may frequently be – in part, at least – a vehicle for the expression of the poet's own personal feelings. There is no love-lyric in this sense in Sanskrit. The whole attitude and training of the Indian poet was such that the idea of using poetry to express the poet's own private feelings hardly ever occurred to him, and probably never in the case of love; nor would he have seen the point of addressing a poem To His Mistress as part of the technique of wooing. This situation may to some extent be due to the fact that he was composing in an elaborate, and in many ways artificial, language of learning, which may not be the ideal type of medium to express emotions which come 'straight from the heart'. But the more important point, really, is that the romantic conception of private, personal poetry (which is in any case often a development harmful to literature) was not among the cultural attitudes of the times. In general, it can be said that Sanskrit love-verses are verses about love, not the verses of a lover. This is so even if the poem may be quite impassioned, and composed in the first person. In such cases, the poet is simply performing the work of a dramatist. Indeed, as we have already remarked, many of the verses in the anthologies are taken from dramas in the first place.

In the poetical treatment of love, Sanskrit poets were frequently unashamedly frank about details of physical passion between lovers; and it would falsify the picture if, from motives of prudery, we were to attempt to disguise this fact in the translations. I should prefer not to use the designation 'erotic', since this term seems to me to have acquired in English some undesirable overtones which would not be justified in relation to most of such verses in Sanskrit. With remarkably few exceptions, sexual love is treated by the poets with delicacy and good taste. Vulgarity in any form is severely criticized in treatises on poetic theory. It is said, for example, that the poet should never use in poetry the verb *yabh-* (a word which in Sanskrit is as vulgar as its four-letter translation in English) – or, as one writer delicately puts it, 'a poet should avoid the use of the word which begins with *y-*'.[1] In spite of this counsel, there is one verse included in the present anthology which does contain the offending word; but, after some debate with myself, I admit, I have in the end decided to replace it in the translation with a less offensive paraphrase, excusing myself on the grounds that this is in accord with the majority opinion of Sanskrit poets and theorists. The same verse also contains an obscene pun, linguistically resistant, however, to translation into English. In an exceptional case like this, I can do no more than apologize if the reader should feel that the point of the original has been somewhat frustrated.

Metres and rhyming effects

The metres of classical Sanskrit are strict. Like those of Greek and Latin, they are based on quantity, and are governed by very similar principles: a syllable with a long vowel or diphthong is always metrically long ('heavy'), as is also a syllable with a short vowel followed by a cluster of two or more consonants, not necessarily within the same word; while a syllable is metrically short ('light') only if it contains a short vowel followed by not more than one consonant. But whereas Latin and Greek admit an option in certain cases, so that a short vowel before groups such as *cr-*, *tr-*, can count either as a metrically long or a metrically short syllable, Sanskrit on the other hand allows no such option, and in all such cases the syllable must count as long. So far as I know, there is only one well attested exception to this in the classical period, and not more than two other doubtful cases; and these were all apparently so shocking to the scribes that many of the manuscripts of the verses in question have

1. I remember seeing some years ago a translation of this by a modern Indian writer – I forget now who – where the sentence was misconstrued as 'a poet should not use words beginning with the letter *y*' – as if we were to counsel English poets to exclude from their verses all words beginning with *f-*.

resorted to scribal emendations to get rid of the irregularity. Again, Latin and Greek frequently have the option of two short syllables in place of one long syllable; and again, except in the Āryā group of metres, Sanskrit cannot accept any such option. The composition of metrically correct verses in Sanskrit is therefore very much more difficult than is the case in Latin or Greek.

The simplest of the classical metres – and consequently the one used almost universally in the non-literary epics, the Purāṇas, unpoetical religious tracts such as the Bhagavad-gītā, and didactic verse generally – is the *anuṣṭubh*.[1] In the most frequent pattern, each half-verse has the form:

• • • • | ∪ — — • | • • — • | ∪ — ∪ •,

where the syllables marked • can be either long or short.[2] This metre is also used not infrequently in real poetry; and in the hands of a master poet such as Kālidāsa, the effect can be so startlingly different from the epic and religious doggerel that it is sometimes hard to believe that it is the same metre.

In the majority of the classical metres, however, the quantity of every syllable (except the final anceps) is rigidly determined. Typically, the stanza consists of four lines of the same metrical shape. There are approximately fifty such metres recognized, with quarter-stanzas ranging from four to twenty-

1. This is the metre which is, in Sanskrit very rarely, but by Western writers almost universally, called the *śloka*-metre: a most unsatisfactory and misleading terminology, since the word *śloka* means simply 'stanza', irrespective of the metre of the stanza.

2. Several variations from this pattern are admissible, subject however to strict rules, so that, for example, the permitted divergences in the second foot impose restrictions on the quantities in the first foot; and if the eleventh syllable is short, the twelfth no longer has the option, but must in this case also be short. It will be noted that, as in Latin and Greek, the final syllable of a metrical line can normally be a *syllaba anceps*.

six syllables, although, in practice, verses with less than eight syllables or more than twenty-one syllables in the line are extremely rare. And among the twenty or thirty metres which one might reasonably expect to meet in a medieval anthology, there are only a dozen or so which occur with high frequency, and which were obviously the favourites of the poets.

The following is an example of the *śārdūla-vikrīḍita*[1] metre, which is one of the most frequently employed of the longer metres:

— — — ∪ ∪ — ∪ — ∪ ∪ ∪ — | — — ∪ — — ∪ —

raktāśoka kṛśodarī kva nu gatā tyaktvānuraktaṃ janaṃ
no dṛṣṭeti mudhaiva cālayasi yad vātābhibhūtaṃ śiraḥ:
utkaṇṭhāghaṭamānaṣaṭpadaghaṭāsaṃghaṭṭaghṛṣṭacchadas
tatpādāhatim antareṇa bhavataḥ puṣpodgamo 'yaṃ kutaḥ.

Paraphrased in an English approximation to the same metre:

Flame-flower crimson Ashóka-tree, where has she gone?
Why left she this heart aflame?
No, then! Say you, you saw her not? Ah, but you lie,
Winds force your proud head to shake.
Bee-swarms, swarming aloft, alust, cluster in clouds,
Crave nectar, yet fail to swarm:
Could such bounty of blooms abound, but for her touch,
Thus rich to enflower your crown?

Now and again, attempts have been made by classical scholars (occasionally even by poets) to imitate in English verse the quantitative metres of Latin and Greek. Without exception, the examples which I have seen of this are complete failures. With this in mind, therefore, I have deliberately chosen for the present example a turgid, fustian Sanskrit verse, where I can with some

1. The name of the metre can be translated as 'Tigers at play', and many of the other classical metres have similarly pleasant names; but the reasons for the choice of such designations as the names of metres are lost in the mists of Indian time.

confidence feel that the translation is not worse as poetry; and the reader can therefore leave literary considerations on one side, and regard this merely as a metrical illustration.

Only on very rare occasions can we hope to be able to imitate at all closely in translation any of the Sanskrit metres. One of the very few examples in the present volume (in the dramatic excerpt from Kālidāsa's *Vikramorvaśīya*) is the following, in the *drutavilambita* metre:

∪ ∪ ∪ — ∪ ∪ — ∪ ∪ — ∪ —

tvayi nibaddharateḥ priyavādinaḥ
praṇayabhangaparāṅmukhacetasaḥ:
kam aparādhalavaṃ mama paśyasi
tyajasi mānini dāsajanaṃ yataḥ.

Ever for you is my love, ever constant, kind.
Never unfaithful: a heart ever true I gave.
Tell me, my darling – forgiveness I pray to find –
Where is the fault that you found in your humble slave?

In the excerpt from the *Kumāra-sambhava*, where the Sanskrit is in the *upajāti* form of the *indravajrā/upendravajrā* metre:

• — ∪ — — ∪ ∪ — ∪ — •

I have tried (partly by the use of feminine rhymes) to convey something of the rhythmical feel of the original stanzas, although without attempting to force the English into an exactly equivalent metrical form.

Here and there, in a very few of the other verses in the anthology, the English version has some reminiscences of the rhythm of the originals; but for the most part, I have been content to choose an English verse-form which seemed appropriate to the sense and atmosphere in any given case, without too strict a regard to the original metre. At the same time, I have tried, by varying the metres and styles of the translations, to give some impression of the fact that the originals do show considerable variations, both in style and in metre.

In the later Indo-Aryan languages, as in the later languages of western Europe, rhyme became a regular feature of verse. Sanskrit, on the other hand, like Latin and Greek, did not normally use rhyme. Nevertheless, assonances, alliterations, and similar effects, are extremely common, and frequently contribute to the charm of the sound of the verse; and end-rhymes (or approximate rhymes), though less common, are occasionally employed to advantage. The following verse (no. 19 in the translations) may illustrate how extremely complex and subtle the sound-patterns can sometimes be:

iNDīvareṇa nayanaṃ mukham aMBujEna
kuNDena daNTam adharaṃ navapallavEna:
aNGāni caMPakadalaiḥ sa vidhāya vEdhāḥ
kāNTe kathaṄ-Ghaṭitavān upalena cEtaḥ.

Here the first two lines rhyme, and the second pair approximately; while in addition the penultimate vowel is the same in all four lines. By the use of capital letters, I have drawn attention to the way in which each line has at the beginning a group of nasal plus plosive, and how this feature is in each case picked up again later in the line, and, except for the first line, in identical position. The recurring *-ena* is of course an inflexional ending, and is thus required for the grammatical structure; but, even so, it also contributes to the incantatory sound-effect of the verse. And further, there are the alliterations: *nd, ṇ, n, n; m, m, mb: nd, n, d, nt, dh, n: d, v-dh, v-dh: k, k, gh.*

A type of rhyming on a grand scale, either internal or at the ends of lines, was also developed, to which the name *yamaka* 'twinning' was applied. For example:

ka*malinīm alinī* dayitaṃ vinā
na *sahate saha te*na niṣevitām:
ta*m adhunā madhunā* nihitaṃ hṛdi
sma*rati sā rati-sā*ram ahar-niśam.

Although such verbal cleverness was highly regarded, it was

naturally seldom successful in high poetry if used too frequently; and writers on the theory of poetry sometimes counsel against the use of *yamakas* in serious poetry, and especially in love-poetry, on the grounds that the purely intellectual effort involved can all too easily distract the poet from his proper concern, which is the conveying of a poetic emotion. But, as always, there are exceptions; and a poet of the stature of Kālidāsa could produce a brilliant verse, where the king Purūravas (in the soliloquy translated in this volume) addresses the peacock:

> nīla*kaṇṭhă* mamot*kaṇṭhā vane* 'smin *vanit*ā tvayā
> dīrgh*āpāṅgā* sit*āpāṅgă dṛṣṭ*ā *dṛṣṭ*ikṣamā bhavet.

In addition to the *yamakas*, observe the rhyming vowel in *nīla-*, *dīrgha-*; and the cross-rhyming *nīlakaṇṭhă* to *sitāpāṅgă* (reinforced by the fact that *nīla* 'blue' and *sita* 'white' are both colour-adjectives); and *mamotkaṇṭhā* to *dīrghāpāṅgā* (with *dīrgha* 'long', and *utkaṇtha*, which might be paraphrased as 'stretched with longing'); and paralleled in the second half of each line by *vane*: *bhavet*, and *tvayā*: *dṛṣṭā*. In the fourth of Brahms's St Antony Variations, there appears a triple counterpoint inverted in the 12th, and, consequently for the other voice, in the 9th, the latter being theoretically virtually hopeless of success. With Brahms, however, it is here miraculously successful, and Professor Donald Tovey commented on it, 'Brahms probably did not figure this out at all but profited by the luck which goes with genius.' Doubtless the same comment would be justified with regard to some of Kālidāsa's verbal effects, which give a similar impression of that effortless mastery which is characteristic of genius.

At the other end of the scale, examples are not lacking of verbal ingenuity which can hardly be considered as poetry, even by the most liberal and kindly of critics. A single specimen will suffice, a verse often quoted in this connexion, where the first line contains no consonants other than *s* and *m*, the second only *y* and *t* (printed here without spacing between the words, in accord with the normal practice of Sanskrit manuscripts):

samesamāsamomāsassāmemāsasamāsamā
yoyātayātayāyātiyāyātyāyātayātayā.

It is not impossible to paraphrase the sense in a little English verse:

When you're away,
A day's a year:
But when you're here,
A year's a day.

But we must admit that the pride of the original author was in the clever form, and that the sense of the verse was of little importance to him. We need not, of course, despise such things: within their own society, they provided a type of amusement similar to that which some of our contemporaries derive from the crossword-puzzle.

Rājaśekhara's prescription for the poetic life

In the tenth chapter of his treatise on poetry, *Kāvya-mīmāṃsā* ('An Enquiry into Poetry'), Rājaśekhara, writing at the beginning of the tenth century A.D., has something to say on the day-to-day life of the poet. First, of course, the poet must have had a sound training, including the thorough study of the dictionaries, treatises on metre and poetic theory, as well as a good general cultural education; and he requires a sound constitution, inspiration, assiduous practice, social contacts with critics of good taste, and so forth. And he should be pure – pure in word, thought, and in body. The first two items are the natural result of his education; while 'purity of body', continues Rājaśekhara, means that his toe-nails should be kept trimmed, that he should chew betel, and use perfume in moderation, wear clothes that are expensive but not ostentatious, and bedeck his head with flowers. He should have a ready smile and a persuasive tongue. He should restrain himself from criticizing the works of other poets, unless he is asked for his opinion; but if his opinion is asked, he should speak the truth candidly (dangerous counsel, this). He should have a house large enough to have rooms suitable for the climate of the various seasons, and it should be kept clean and tidy; and it should have a garden, where he can rest among the trees, with a hillock for games, a lotus-pond and streams, with peacocks, deer and doves, herons, ducks and geese, ospreys, parrots, and other birds. The house should be well-constructed to keep cool in the hot season, and should have baths and showers, and other luxuries. Things should be so arranged as to ensure that, when he has become somewhat stale after too strenuous a spell of poetic composition, his servants should know to go about their duties in silence, or leave him entirely undisturbed while he recuperates.

Since a routine is necessary for efficiency, he should divide the day as well as the night into four parts. After rising and saying his morning prayers, and a hymn to Sarasvatī (the goddess of poetry), he should retire to his study, and, making himself comfortable, should engage in study of the ancillary sciences, lexicography, metrics, and so forth, until the end of the first quarter of the day. The second quarter should be devoted to poetic composition. Then about midday, a bath and a meal. After lunch, until the end of the third quarter of the day, he should meet and converse with literary friends, with whom he can discuss literary criticism, or on occasion engage in the pastime of extempore verse-completion (see verses 146–51 in this volume). Then, in the last part of the day he should revise what he has composed in the morning, either by himself or with the benefit of the criticism of one or two close friends. After evening prayers, a fair copy should be made of the day's composition; and then for the remainder of the first quarter of the night, he may if he is so inclined seek feminine company, and make love. The second and third quarters of the night are to be devoted to sleep; for nothing, says Rājaśekhara, is so important for the maintenance of good health as good, sound sleep. Finally, in the last watch of the night he should rise, and (a small matter which apparently had been overlooked at the beginning of the account) attend to any other business he might have, while he is still fresh.

It is not to be imagined that many Sanskrit poets were fortunate enough to be able to devote their lives to poetry in this fashion; and we may suspect that this account describes how Rājaśekhara himself would have liked to live, rather than how poets usually did live. In his case, it is true, it might have been possible, since he is known to have been a comparatively wealthy man. But poetry was not a highroad to economic prosperity; and while many poets undoubtedly found royal patronage, or were themselves kings or ministers of state, there must have been many more who were less fortunate: Brahmans with little wealth other than their Sanskritic learning.

At this point, I should have liked to provide for those who are interested some information about some of the individual poets. But in most cases nothing is known of them as persons, and little of interest could be said.

And in any case, the Prologue has already held the stage for long enough: *alam ativistareṇa* – without further prolixity, I leave it to the poems, to speak for themselves.

Interwelded as words and meaning
  Pārvatī and the Lord of Lords,
Parents, masters of all the earth:
  Grant inspired meaning to my words.

How can the poet's slender powers
  Deal justly with so large a theme?
Why should I think that I can cross
  The ocean in a coracle?

A fool to seek a poet's fame,
  Shall I win only ridicule?
Tall men can scarcely reach the fruit:
  A dwarf, I stretch my arms in vain.

Yet, where the ancient poets cut
  The gateway, I may enter in.
Where diamond pierced the way, a pearl
  Is threaded by the softest thread.

Kālidāsa

I

1

Is poetry always worthy when it's old?
And is it worthless, then, because it's new?
Reader, decide yourself if this be true:
Fools suspend judgement, waiting to be told.

Kālidāsa

If learned critics publicly deride
My verse, well, let them. Not for them I wrought.
One day a man shall live to share my thought:
For time is endless and the world is wide.

Bhavabhūti

2

Of what use is the poet's poem,
    Of what use is the bowman's dart,
Unless another's senses reel
    When it sticks quivering in the heart?

3

Scoundrels without the wit to fit
A word or two of verse together
Are daunted not a whit to sit
In judgement on the abstruse poetry of another.
Such men will listen with attentive mind,
Alert to see how many faults they find.
And if they're vexed because they fail to grasp the sense
Of works conceived for readers of intelligence,
They naturally do not blame their foolishness:
A girl who's less than perfect always blames the dress.

4

A man lives long who lives a hundred years:
Yet half is sleep, and half the rest again
Old age and childhood. For the rest, a man
Lives close companion to disease and tears,
Losing his love, working for other men.
Where can joy find a space in this short span?

Bhartṛhari

5

Blow, wind, to where my loved one is,
  Touch her, and come and touch me soon:
I'll feel her gentle touch through you,
  And meet her beauty in the moon.
These things are much for one who loves –
  A man can live by them alone –
That she and I breathe the same air,
  And that the earth we tread is one.

(*Rāmāyaṇa*)

6

'Do not go', I could say; but this is inauspicious.
'All right, go' is a loveless thing to say.
'Stay with me' is imperious. 'Do as you wish' suggests
Cold indifference. And if I say 'I'll die
When you are gone', you might or might not believe me.
Teach me, my husband, what I ought to say
When you go away.

7

Today adds yet another day
And still your father is unkind.
The darkness closes up the path.
Come, little son, let us go to bed.

8

No single plant in this world's garden-plot
Bears such sweet fruit, such bitter fruit as she:
Ambrosial are the apples on her tree
When she's in love, and poison when she's not.

Bhartṛhari

9

You cheat yourself and others with your lies,
Philosopher, so foolish-wise,
In that you state
A celibate
Has greater grace to win the prize.
Are there not heavenly nymphs beyond the skies?

Bhartṛhari

10

Although my mind
Is sick with love, I find
I have acquired the gift of magic sight.
Though she is far away, and it is night,
I see her in a foreign land
From where I stand.

11

Upwards, thick cloud-tresses, and below them
  the mountain-slopes where the peacock plays;
See, on the ground snow flower-petal whiteness:
  where shall the traveller rest his gaze?

Bhartṛhari

12

The clear bright flame of man's discernment dies
When a girl clouds it with her lamp-black eyes.

Bhartṛhari

13

Her face is not the moon, nor are her eyes
Twin lotuses, nor are her arms pure gold:
She's flesh and bone. What lies the poets told!
Ah, but we love her, we believe the lies.

Bhartṛhari

14

If the forest of her hair
Calls you to explore the land,
And her breasts, those mountains fair,
Tempt that mountaineer, your hand –
  Stop! before it is too late:
  Love, the brigand, lies in wait.

Bhartṛhari

15

She needeth no instruction in the art
Of using woman's wiles to win man's heart:
The lily's scarlet stamens grew untaught,
The bee came freely, wishing to be caught.

Bhartṛhari

16

With dancing starry eyes the face of night
Was captured by the moon's first rising flush:
The darkness-cloak that quelled the sunset's blush
Fell from her, unperceived, before his sight.

17

In former days we'd both agree
That you were me, and I was you.
What has now happened to us two,
That you are you, and I am me?

Bhartṛhari

18

This is the truth, good people, and no lie.
Why should I lie? In heaven, and earth, and hell,
Womman is mannes blis and al his joye:
Womman is mannes onlie grief as wel.

Bhartṛhari

19

After God made your eyes of lotus-blue,
Took for your teeth white jasmine, shaped the whole
Face as a better lily, chose the hue
And texture of magnolia for your skin,
He then grew tired of soft things, and within
He carved from flint the impenetrable soul.

20

Love goes a-fishing with the rod Desire,
Baiting his hook with Woman for delight.
Attracted by the flesh, the men-fish bite.
He hauls them in and cooks them in his fire.

Bhartṛhari

21

The ugly vulture eats the dead,
Guiltless of murder's taint.
The heron swallows living fish
And looks like an ascetic saint.

22

Earrings for sale in the village here?
Goldsmith, you'll not sell many, I fear.
Hasn't the news yet got around
That nothing pierces the headman's ear?

23

Granted her breasts are firm, her face entrancing,
Her legs enchanting – what is that to you?
My mind, if you would win her, stop romancing.
Have you not heard, reward is virtue's due?

Bhartṛhari

24

You are pale, friend moon, and do not sleep at night,
And day by day you waste away.
Can it be that you also
Think only of her, as I do?

25

Has God no pity, while he counts away
The endless hours of every weary day,
The endless nights, when still my sad head lies
Unpillowed by the breast of Lotus-eyes?

26

No, but look here now, this is just absurd,
The way our famous poets talk of girls
As weak and winsome. Weak? Is this a word
To use of those who, with a shake of curls
And with the triumph of a modest glance,
Can lead the very gods a merry dance?

Bhartṛhari

27

On sunny days there in the shade
Beneath the trees reclined a maid
Who lifted up her dress (she said)
To keep the moonbeams off her head.

Bhartṛhari

28

Of Amor is yone hure ane altir fyre
Quhair passioun ay kyndillis het desyre,
That yhongis thair evir sacrifices heilth
Offrand oblacioun of yewth and weilth.

Bhartṛhari

29

A flock of blackbirds, and a crow
As black as those he walks among;
And which is which you'd scarcely know
If he would only hold his tongue.

30

They say the god of love
  has flowers for darts
And that the moon above
  is cold and chill:
I am a wretch for whom
  this works but ill.
There is but little room
  in lovers' hearts
To bear such freezing rays
  that burn and blaze
Or to survive a flower
  of lightning power.

Kālidāsa

31

This flower unsmelt, this opening bud unplucked,
This unpierced jewel, new honey, sweet, untasted,
This perfect form, this whole reward of heaven
– What man is worthy to enjoy this treasure?

Kālidāsa

32

Vallisneria may intertwine
  yet the lotus shows its grace;
Speckled dirt upon the moon's cold face
  makes that beauty brighter shine.
So the covering of a hermit's dress
  still reveals her loveliness.
Beauty's own true form can always bring
  ornament from anything.

Kālidāsa

33

Regent divine of joy's own treasury,
Home of all beauty's essences combined –
Who could have made her but the god of love
With moonlight's nectar stamens intertwined?

Bhavabhūti

34

When God made me, why did he then conspire
To make her beauty? If both had to be,
Why did he then make spring to wake desire?
  Surely he made the spring to break
  Men's hearts: but why then did he make
The mango-blossom on the mango-tree?

35

When the East
Gave birth to the Moon,
Love was the dancer at the feast;
The heavens smiled for joy;
And the Wind strewed the perfumed dust
Of lotus-pollen in the courtyard of the sky.

Dharmakīrti

36

'The road is rough; and, oh, the moon is bright
  – Suppose my husband should discover!
People may talk. – But can I bear tonight
  To disappoint my lover?'
And so she walked a step or two, and then
  Turned and came back again.

37

You're off to meet your lover in some haste,
  With tinkling necklaces and bangles,
A merry girdle clinking at your waist,
  While at each step an anklet jangles.
(You glance around in constant trepidation,
Fearful of coming under observation.)

Amaru

38

He counted not the cost of beauty's grace,
But toiled for a perfected work of art;
And so she kindles a contented heart
To fever by the vision of her face.
Her sad perfection, matchless and apart,
Finds no fit counterpart. With what intention
Did God take thought to shape this fair invention?

Dharmakīrti

39

Who was artificer at her creation?
Was it the moon, bestowing its own charm?
Was it the graceful month of spring, itself
Compact with love, a garden full of flowers?
That ancient saint there, sitting in his trance,
Bemused by prayers and dull theology,
Cares naught for beauty: how could *he* create
Such loveliness, the old religious fool?

Kālidāsa

40

The moon tries every month in vain
To paint a picture of your face;
And, having failed to catch its grace,
Destroys the work, and starts again.

41

Because she's been compared to you,
The proud moon lifts her head on high.
How little she has understood,
My lady with the downcast eyes.

42

Poor, foolish man! who, in his verses, thought
The moon was, for his lady's face,
The ideal simile he sought!
Or did the moon then smile? or frown? or move
Man's heart with laughter? tears? or any trace
Of love?

43

All men alike have suffered theft:
If a man sees her, she will steal his heart;
Yet, if he sees her not, what has he left
Worth looking at?

44

The grammar-books all say that 'mind' is neuter,
And so I thought it safe to let my mind
Salute her.
But now it lingers in embraces tender:
For Pāṇini made a mistake, I find,
In gender.

Dharmakīrti

45

A hundred times I learnt from my philosophy
To think no more of love, this vanity,
This dream, this source of all regret,
This emptiness.
But no philosophy can make my heart forget
Her loveliness.

Dharmakīrti

46

'Ah, she is fair', you say; 'her tender eyes – '
You say; 'her lotus-blossom face – ' you say;
'Her budding breasts – ' you say. For shame, my heart.
This is vain torture. Would you seek to drink
At a mirage? No, never again, I say,
Shall you encourage dallying thoughts of love
To find a foothold on forbidden paths.

Dharmakīrti

47

Although I have a lamp, and fire,
Stars, moon, and sun to give me light,
Unless I look into her eyes,
All is black night.

Bhartṛhari

48

The night that's past will not return to me.
The Jumna's floods flow onward to the sea.

49

The pleasant city and its mighty king,
The tributary princes at his side,
The learned men that were the kingdom's pride,
The minstrels with a ready song to sing,
The gracious ladies of the court, the ring
Of haughty nobles, arrogant of birth,
Are conquered by the Lord of all the earth,
Time, who makes memories of everything.

Bhartṛhari

50

Destiny surely is unjust.
The bees, it has decreed,
Shall feast on lotus-honey and sweet pollen-dust.
On water-weed
The geese must
Feed.

51

It may be hard enough to do,
  But if you try, you'll find
A way to pin down quicksilver,
  But not a woman's mind.

52

Strong drink may make a man forget
  His mother or his wife,
Mistake a palace for the shack
  He's lived in all his life.
One day, a puddle is the sea;
  The next, he'll try to stand
Upon the ocean's surface, which
  To him appears dry land,
To such a drunkard's foolishness
  There's hardly any end:
He'll even think, when he's in drink,
  A king might be a friend.

53

The great autumnal clouds pour rain
And cool the fever of our summer pain.
Do great lords gather riches, then,
To ease the suffering of their fellow-men?

54

Those whom the gods would keep
In safety, they protect,
Not as a shepherd guards his sheep,
But by the gift of a wise intellect.

Nor do the gods appear
In warrior's armour clad
To strike men down with sword or spear.
Those whom they would destroy, they
first make mad.

55

Wise men will cherish more than all
Jove's nectar haughty men's despite.
The lowly sleep in peace at night:
Pride lies awake and fears a fall.

56

My lord, since you have banished Poverty
From this fair land, I feel it is my duty
To lay an information that the outlaw
Has taken refuge in my humble home.

57

Eild has my eyne clokit in darknes,
My fors is failyeit in distres
And feblit with infermite:
This warld is verray vanite.
Sen Deid hes all my brether tane,
In this warld I man lif alane:
Thocht plesour mair I myght nat se,
Timor mortis conturbat me.

Bhartṛhari

58

A man speaks harsh words against me:
I forgive him,
And go on my way rejoicing.
But then I am sad again
To think that I was the cause
Of this regrettable lapse
From good manners.

59

ahāny astamayāntāni udayāntā ca śarvarī
sukhasyāntaṃ sadā duḥkhaṃ duḥkhasyāntaṃ sadā sukham.

So nixt to summer winter bein;
Nixt efter confort cairis kein;
  Nixt dirk mednycht the mirthefull morrow;
  Nixt efert joy aye cumis sorrow:
So is this warld and ay hes bein.

q dumbar

60

The impudence of some people,
To say such things about an honest woman!
'Stop thief!' cries the burglar,
And carries on breaking in.

61

Most men can see another's faults;
Another's virtues some can see;
And there are those who see their own
Shortcomings. Yes? – Well, – two or three.

62

Slender at first, they quickly gather force,
Growing in richness as they run their course;
Once started, they do not turn back again:
Rivers, and years, and friendships with good men.

63

Fate, give me any other ill you please:
I'll bear it gladly. But I live among
Men who are philistines: do not mark me then
To be a poet, do not mark me, do not mark me.

64

'Stop but a moment, friend, and rise and carry
The burden of my weary poverty.'
But the dead man, who would not change his peace
For poverty, said nothing in reply.

65

'I see that a little person
Who has obtained a high situation
Very easily falls from it,'
Said the pebble,
As a breath of wind dislodged it
From the mountain-top.

66

The noble man works for another's good,
Sacrificing his own. Most common men
Will help another, if it's understood
That nothing of their own is thereby lost.
Devils incarnate we can comprehend,
Those who wax fat while others bear the cost.
But are there wretches who would harm a friend
And neighbour without any hope of gain?

Bhartṛhari

67

Peaceful, the gentle deer untroubled graze:
All that they need, their forest-home supplies.
No greed for wealth nor envy clouds their days.
But these are only beasts, and we are wise.

68

The summer sun, who robbed the pleasant nights,
And plundered all the water of the rivers,
And burned the earth, and scorched the forest-trees,
Is now in hiding; and the autumn clouds,
Spread thick across the sky to track him down,
Hunt for the criminal with lightning-flashes.

69

Where are you going in the dead of night?
'To meet my lover who is life and death to me.'
And are you not afraid to walk alone?
'How can I be alone? Love keeps me company.'

Amaru

70

Patience, better than armour, guards from harm.
And why seek enemies, if you have anger?
With friends, you need no medicine for danger.
With kinsmen, why ask fire to keep you warm?
What use are snakes when slander sharper stings?
What use is wealth where wisdom brings content?
With modesty, what need for ornament?
With poetry's Muse, why should we envy kings?

Bhartṛhari

71

Deer and fish and good men live
On grass and water and content:
No cause for hatred do they ever give
To hunters, fishers, or to men malevolent.

Bhartṛhari

72

Love made a magic snare –
My lady's arms. When they're not there,
My breath comes short, I pant and choke with pain;
But when they tighten round my neck, I live again.

73

Trees bend when the fruit swells.
With fresh rains, the clouds droop low.
Good men are not made proud by wealth.
They cannot act otherwise:
It is their nature to bring help to others.

74

Seeking shelter from the sun,
A bald man sat beneath a Bilva-tree.
A fruit fell down
And cracked his crown.
It often happens that an unfortunate man is followed by misfortunes wherever he goes.

Bhartṛhari

75

Prince, would you milk this bounteous cow, the State?
First, you must let the People drink their share:
Only when calves are fed, will Earth's tree bear
Fruit, like a cornucopia, for your plate.

Bhartṛhari

76

When I knew a little, then I was like an elephant blinded with rut, and my mind was infected by the pride of omniscience: but when from wise men I learned and understood a little here and a little there, then I knew I was a fool, and my pride vanished like a fever cured.

Bhartṛhari

77

From all your herds, a cup or two of milk,
From all your granaries, a loaf of bread,
In all your palace, only half a bed:
Can man use more? And do you own the rest?

78

Flaunt your proud head, moon. Nightingale, arise
And sing. Wake, lotus, spread your petals wide.
My lady who has vanquished all your pride
Is gently sleeping, silent, with closed eyes.

79

Although I conquer all the earth,
Yet for me there is only one city.
In that city there is for me only one house;
And in that house, one room only;
And in that room, a bed.
And one woman sleeps there,
The shining joy and jewel of all my kingdom.

80

Strike me, and try me to your heart's content
With fire and touchstone: I accept my fate.
But oh I bitterly resent
The fact that you should weigh me with a pennyweight.

81

'Thundercloud, I think you are wicked.
You know I'm going to meet my own lover,
And yet you first scare me with your thunder,
And now you're trying to caress me
With your rain-hands.'

Śūdraka

82

The cure for pride is knowledge. Who can cure
A man who's proud of knowledge? If the patient
Should be allergic to ambrosia,
The prognosis
Is hopeless.

83

A ray is caught in a bowl,
And the cat licks it, thinking that it's milk;
Another threads its way through tree-branches,
And the elephant thinks he has found a lotus-stalk.
Half asleep, a girl reaches out
And tries to rearrange the moonbeams on the bed
To share the warmth.
It is the moon that is drunk with its own light,
But the world that is confused.

84

Slowly the darkness drains away the sunlight.
Drawn homeward to their nests, the crows fall silent.
And now the owl sits in the hollow tree,
Bolder, neck sunk inside his body,
And stares; swivels his head; and stares.

85

A poet's song
Sings in the hearts of poets: the common throng
Does not respond.
The ocean's swell
Wakes to the moon: do tides rise in a well
Or muddy pond?

86

I know, sweet honey-throat, cuckoo,
Your voice is mere hypocrisy:
As soon as you have wings to fly
You leave the birds that fostered you.

87

Dearest, if you will love me true,
What use are joys of heaven to me?
But if you will not love me true,
What use are joys of heaven to me?

88

The open-handed have the tighter fist:
They take their hoarded merits when they go.
The mean man is your true philanthropist:
When dead, he leaves his total wealth below.

89

Ah, Poverty, I mourn for your sad fate.
So long ago you claimed me as your friend,
And ever since have been my constant guest.
Where will you find a home when I am dead?

Śūdraka

90

[*Now she is asleep; and I can sit and watch her beauty.*]

She is Heaven's blessing in my house,
She is a salve of nectar to my eyes.
Her cool hands when they touch my body
Refresh and comfort more than any liquid sandal.
Her arms around my neck are smooth as snow,
Lovely as pearl-lustre.
How can she ever bring me anything but happiness?
  – Except for one thing.
How could I ever bear her loss?

Bhavabhūti

91

The fire of envious critics' tongues
Refines the true poetic gold.
Should we not celebrate in cheerful songs
Poor fools who give us benefits untold?

Varāhamihira

92

At night the rain came, and the thunder deep
Rolled in the distance; and he could not sleep,
But tossed and turned, with long and frequent sighs,
And as he listened, tears came to his eyes;
And thinking of his young wife left alone,
He sobbed and wept aloud until the dawn.
And from that time on
The villagers made it a strict rule that no traveller should be allowed to take a room for the night in the village.

Amaru

93

Weaving by Penelope,
My girl sipping her *café*:
Women always can produce
Some excuse.

94

'Won't you awake and eat?' I gently said:
But still she slept, though opening half an eye,
Then straightway closed it. Turning with a sigh
She nestled warmly deeper in the bed.

95

Rise early, son,
Ponder your acts, think of the world to come:
For, be assured, the fruits of all you do
Will think on you.

96

When he saw her,
He was struck by the arrows of love.
Nor could he save himself by shutting his eyes:
For he was a young man of an enquiring
And philosophical turn of mind.
And so he was forced to examine the problem
In greater detail
Of how the Creator
Had come to make
A figure like hers.

97

Good noble men, after a fall
Bounce like a ball.
Th' ignoble fall another way:
Like lumps of clay.

98

A hundred times they kiss, and then
A thousand times embrace,
And stop only to start again:
There's no tautology in such a case.

99

'Remember me,' – 'But that I cannot do:
The heart which should remember goes with you.'

100

A critic is a creature who has views
Quite like a camel's: flowers and fruit he scorns.
In the flower-garden of the honeyed Muse
He starves unless he finds a meal of thorns.

101

A man who has the world for his wide bed,
His arm for pillow and the sky for tent,
The pleasant wind to fan him, overhead
Bright moon for lamplight, and his calm content
His consort – were it not he lacked one thing,
Life's anxious fear, would sleep like any king.

Bhartṛhari

102

Black clouds at midnight;
Deep thunder rolling.
The night has lost the moon:
A cow lowing for her lost calf.

103

A book, a woman, and a money-loan,
  Once they are gone, are gone.
And better so. – Sometimes they do return:
  Piecemeal; or soiled; or torn.

104

'You are my love and I am yours,' says he;
'Thou art my life, I thine,' so answers she.
    But how
    Can we
    Say 'thou'
    Or 'me'?
In our true lovers' accidence we find
Both words alike regularly declined.

105

'So, friar, I see you have a taste for meat.'
'Not that it's any good without some wine.'
'You like wine too, then?' 'Better when I dine
With pretty harlots.' 'Surely such girls eat
No end of money?' 'Well, I steal, you see,
Or win at dice.' 'A thief and gambler too?'
'Why, certainly. What else is there to do?
Aren't you aware I'm vowed to poverty?'

106

Truly, the loss of wealth is no great pain.
When Fate disposes, wealth begins, or ends.
Yet one heart-burning follows in its train:
The sorrow of the cooling off of friends.

Śūdraka

107

Bee, you fly so far around:
Tell me, have you ever found,
Seen, or ever heard men tell
Of a flower to match the grace
– Speak, and do not fear to tell –
Of the gentle lily's face?

108

At set of sun
Sleep closes up the eyes. But why,
When wealth is gone,
Does man, with equal ease, not die?

109

The sun and moon, for all their light,
Have little reason to be proud,
When he by day and she by night
Share the same ragged patch of cloud.

110

Ascetics, who in woman nothing found
Of virtue, judged her to be wholly bad.
Perhaps, like other critics, they were mad;
And certainly their sentence was not sound.

111

Flamingo, what has brought you here?
Has no-one told you that the cranes
In this land have usurped your name?
Why have you come? Go home again
Before some fool calls you a crane.

112

A poet who has never tasted grief
Can mourn in fiction, and command belief.
A man who mourns in truth has no such art
To find words for a broken heart.

113

If you can look into her wide black eyes
Unmoved, observe her laughing brows and keep
Your wits about you – I express surprise,
But honour you as you deserve, poor sheep.

114

My best respects to Poverty,
The master who has set me free:
For I can look at all the world,
And no-one looks at me.

115

'The night will pass soon, and the dawn will come.
The sun will soon rise, and the lotus open.'
But while the bee dreamt, caught within the blossom,
An elephant uprooted the lotus-plant.

116

While describing to her best friend
Her adventures with her lover,
She realized she was talking to her husband,
And added, 'And then I woke up.'

117

Rags are enough for me, silk pleases you:
A difference undifferentiated.
A man is poor till his desires are sated.
Who is the rich, who poor, between us two?

Bhartṛhari

118

The day is surely better than the night?
Or is the night not better than the day?
How can I tell? But this I know is right:
Both are worth nothing when my love's away.

Amaru

119

'Give me that bit of rag; or take the boy
And try to keep him warm.' 'The ground this side
Is bare, and there's at least some straw at yours.'
The burglar who had quietly entered heard,
Threw over them the ragged cloak he'd lifted
Elsewhere, and crept away again, in tears.

120

A use can be found
For rotten wood,
And infertile ground
May produce some good.
   Kings, when they fall,
   Have no uses at all.

121

Well worth it was the pummelling into shape,
Well worth it the fierce drying sun, and still
Well worth it was the drowning in the slip,
Well worth it the hot firing in the kiln.
No blessing ever comes without some ill.
Now you are cradled in her slender arm,
Held close against her breast, safe from all harm,
And my beloved takes you to the well.

122

To be apart
From you, sweetheart,
May yet be best.
One thing I see
When you're with me,
A single face:
From all things – one.
When you are gone,
I see your grace
In all the rest.

(Or, *if the reader prefers a different style:*)

Pure logic may convince a lover's heart
That ampler blessings flow when we're apart.
When she is here, my lady is but one:
When she's away, in all things I see her alone.

123

Nature can kindle and, unaided, nurse
The fire of love. Must we endure this curse
Of poets who thus needlessly rehearse
Their wretched passion in such wretched verse?

124

Those who seek righteousness will gladly spend
Their hard-earned wealth to gladden foe or friend.
When men delight in chiding my offence,
Have I not gained as much, at less expense?

125

Against a target swift, invisible,
What skilful archer dare display his art?
  Love, without pausing to take aim,
Loosed all his arrows, and none missed my heart.

Harṣa

126

  Water to quench a blaze,
Shade to keep off the sun's fierce light,
Goad for the elephant in rut,
  Stick for the ox and mule,
  Herbs to subdue disease,
Spells for the poison serpent's bite –
All things else have an antidote:
  Nothing can cure a fool.

127

This is her face? Then the moon's tale is told.
And this her lustre? Then alas for gold.
The lotus is made worthless by her eyes:
All nectar's virtues her sweet smile supplies.
When set beside her brows, what is Love's bow?
That the Creator does not plagiarize
His own fair works, these fair examples show.

Rājaśekhara

128

You are the king: we too are highly placed,
Honoured for the deep wisdom we command.
You are praised for your riches: poets sing
Our fame in every corner of the land.
Thus no great difference lies between yourself
And us. – And, sire, if you despise our state,
We for our part care naught for anything.

Bhartṛhari

129

I am no actor, nor a prince's jester,
No king's musician, nor a scheming courtier.
What place at court, then, for a man such as I am?
For neither am I a young attractive woman.

Bhartṛhari

130

There are men brave enough to face and slay
A wild rogue elephant, or a hungry lion.
But – I will tell such heroes to their face –
Few men, for all their strength, can break Love's pride.

131

She who is always in my thoughts prefers
Another man, and does not think of me.
Yet he seeks for another's love, not hers;
And some poor girl is grieving for my sake.
  Why then, the devil take
Both her and him; and love; and her; and me.

Bhartṛhari

132

Moonlight face,
Flower-bud hand,
Nectar voice,
Rose-red lip:
  Stone-hard heart.

133

She fainted when she heard him say
  That he must go abroad; and then,
  Reviving, said, 'You're back again!
My love, you've been so long away.'

134

At dawn the old man, slowly, painfully,
Managed to stand, but trembling at the knees,
Clutching hard fist over stick, while tears met
The dribble from the corner of his mouth,
His scorched and fragment rags barely concealing
A tattered loin-cloth. Forcing crooked legs
To give their utmost paralytic speed,
He started on another day's long road,
Shivering, half-conscious of the bitter wind.

135

'Well, but you surely do not mean to spend
Your whole life pining? Show some proper spirit.
Are there no other men? What is the merit
Of faithfulness to one?' But when her friend
  Gave this advice, she answered, pale with fear,
'Speak soft. My love lives in my heart, and he will hear.'

Amaru

136

Gazelle-eyed maidens, hard to find,
Horses of noble ancestry,
And parasites who do not mind
Contemptuous words, and bards to sing
His paltry praise: all these a king
Buys dearly, and exhausts his treasury.

137

Now surely it is hardly fair
To blame the lotus in your hair.
Dear pretty one, do you not see?
Your own sweet fragrance has bewitched the bee.

138

Earth mocks the man who buries wealth;
Death laughs at him who guards his health:
The secret mocking of a faithless wife
Who laughs to see her husband love her son.

139

The lotus-flower, that once was proud
To match your eyes, is drowned and out of sight.
The moon, reflector of your beauty's light,
Has hid herself behind a cloud.
The wild geese, eager to express
Your grace, have flown away. My grudging Fate
Denies me even such inadequate
Reminders of your loveliness.

Yaśovarman

140

Philosophers are surely wrong to say
That attributes in substance must inhere.
Her beauty burns my heart; yet I am here,
  And she is far away.

141

The pieces move, now few, now more:
Here many, where before was one,
Here none, where many stood before.
Time, with the goddess Death at play,
Sits at the chequer-board and rolls
Alternate dice of night and day,
And takes the pieces: living souls
Of all that dwell beneath the sun.

Bhartṛhari

142

We were one flesh; and then it came to pass
You were the lover whom I loved, alas.
You are my husband now, and I your wife;
Yet my unfeeling heart protracts my life.

Amaru

143

She neither turned away, nor yet began
To speak harsh words, nor did she bar the door;
But looked at him who was her love before
As if he were an ordinary man.

Amaru

144

When the pet parrot in the morning starts
To chatter rather much of what he heard
Of last night's talk between the young sweethearts,
The young wife does her best to check the bird,
Embarrassed that the older folk should hear,
And quickly stops his beak, trying to feed
The creature with a ruby from her ear,
Pretending it's a pomegranate seed.

Amaru

145

The moon knows by how much her beauty fails,
Weighed against yours, to bring the balance even.
Look! In a vain attempt to turn the scales
She adds as makeweights all the stars of heaven.

Murāri

(Just as a musician might be given a theme on which to extemporize a fugue, so a poet might demonstrate his technical skill by meeting the challenge of 'verse-completion' (*samasyā-pūraṇa*), by constructing a stanza to contain a given line or phrase. There was of course a temptation to choose for the challenge-phrase rather improbable material, and occasionally even nonsense syllables, success being judged by the extent to which the poet was able to achieve an effect of ease and spontaneity. In the six examples which follow, the challenge-phrase is given in italics.)

146

A certain maid at Rāma's coronation,
Befuddled by the wine of celebration,
Dropped a gold jug, which down the staircase rang:
Tum-tumty-tum-tum-ta-ta-tumty-tang.

147

When Krishna with Chānūra fought,
Before the latter came to die
His head was spinning, and he thought
A hundred moons were in the sky.

148

Ah, if the moon would cease to shine so fair
When we are far apart, my love and I!
If he would only come, I should not care
Although *a hundred moons were in the sky.*

149

No man, they say, has ever found the place
Where lotus-flowers within a lotus rise.
Yet I have seen two dark blue-lotus eyes
Set in the fair white-lotus of your face.

150

'Well, really, there is nothing I can tell
Of what men do in love; no, not a word:
He started to undo my dress, and – Well,
I swear I can't remember what occurred.'

151

He held her face, and would not let her go:
She tried to say, 'Oh, no! No, no! Oh, no,
No, no!' But through the kiss no sound would come
Except '*Hmm-hmm-hmm hm hm hmm hm hmmmm!*'

152

Girl bouncing a ball

'She strikes the ball, angered that it can dare
To match her breasts', her lotus thinks, and lies
Prostrate and frightened, fallen from her hair,
Beseeching the forgiveness of her eyes.

153

The ignorant are quickly satisfied,
And argument will soon convince the wise;
But Heaven's own wisdom scarcely will suffice
To contradict a half-baked scholar's pride.

Bhartṛhari

154

If only you squeeze hard enough, you will
  Press oil from sand;
And, if you're thirsty, even drink your fill
  From a mirage.
Sooner or later you may somewhere find
  A rabbit's horn:
But never hope to change the stubborn mind
  Of a born fool.

If you can snatch the jewel a crocodile
  Holds in its teeth,
If you can swim across the ocean, while
  The tempest roars,
If round your head, unruffled, you can wind
  A poison snake,
You still can't hope to change the stubborn mind
  Of a born fool.

Bhartṛhari

155

Shun these six faults to win success:
  Sleep, sloth,
  Fear, wrath,
Slovenliness, longwindedness.

156

A teacher failing in his moral teaching,
A priest unscholarly who still is preaching,
A king whose subjects look for help in vain,
A wife whose voice portends a husband's pain,
A shepherd who on urban pleasures broods,
A barber dreaming of the hills and woods,
All six, – avoid them. Every one can be
As lethal as a leaky boat at sea.

157

Medical advice

When the fever is caused by her looks and her voice,
  The treatment of choice
  Is a thrice-daily sip
  Of her honey-sweet lip.
  To avoid further harm,
  And to keep the heart warm,
This follow-up treatment is known to be best:
The soothing and gentle warm touch of her breast.
  (Professional secret, though –
  Careful to keep it so!)

158

Take not in hand your mango-feathered dart,
Love, do not string your bow
To strike in thoughtless sport my fainting mind –
Surely heroic prey!
Why do you, Love? Already in my heart
Blazing from long ago
The fire was lit by her soft glance, unkind,
And burned that heart away.

Jayadeva

159

She is sweet to enjoy, she is fair, she is fine,
Pretty girl, and in love, she is lovely and more.
Oh, she lives in my heart, she's the one I adore;
Never fasting or prayers won a heaven such as mine.

2

From KĀLIDĀSA'S *VIKRAMORVAŚĪYA*

The theme of the drama is the love of the mortal king Purūravas for the heavenly nymph Urvashī. The legend is an old one, and a rather grimmer form of it is alluded to, though not narrated in detail, in the Vedic literature. In Kālidāsa's version it has been transformed into a gentler, romantic tale. In Act 1, the king rescued the nymph from the demon Keshin and his army who were seeking to abduct her: the second verse in the following extract refers to this event.

At the beginning of Act 4, Urvashī, jealous because the king has happened to glance at a fairy-girl, rushes off into the forest, and by mischance enters a sacred grove forbidden to women; and as a punishment she is straightway changed into a creeper. The king, distracted with grief, wanders around the forest looking for her, and in the following soliloquy asks for information from the various forest creatures. At the end of the extract, he finally encounters the creeper in question, having by then in his hand the magic stone which has power to change Urvashī back to her original form.

The alternation of prose and verses is typical of Sanskrit drama in general. The present scene, in one group of manuscripts, is interlarded with additional verses in Prakrit or Apabhraṃśa, some to be sung by the king, some as comments on the action, presumably intended to be sung as in the manner of a Greek chorus. The authenticity of these verses has been much debated; but there can be no doubt that they are late interpolations, and represent a re-working of the scene centuries later than Kālidāsa, for a sort of operatic adaptation. These later songs, therefore, are omitted in the translation.

[*Enter the King, as one deranged.*] Accursed demon, stop, you devil, stop. Where are you taking my darling to? Ah . . . –

Look! From the mountain top he has leapt into the sky: he rains down arrows upon me. [*Pausing to reflect.*]

Only a storm-cloud, thunder-girt:
No demon arrogant, though armed to smite.
A rainbow – not a tight-bent war-bow there.
Only fierce rain: why should it hurt?
Here are no arrows. And that golden light –
Mere lightning-flashes, not my love's gold hair.

[*Pensively.*] But where, where could she have gone?

Might she have vanished, if I caused her harm?
Swift would I be forgiven.
Goddess she is: might she fly home to heaven?
No, her heart's love is warm.
The devil hosts, once, I reduced to flight,
And saved my lovely one.
She is lost, lost now: what has Fortune done
To hide her from my sight?

[*Looking at the sky, and sighing.*] Ah, when Fate averts her face from men, sorrow treads on the heels of sorrow:

At one stroke, she is gone,
Leaving me hard and bitter pain:
And now new clouds must bring the rain,
Cooling sweet days after the scorching sun.

[*Ironically.*] No, but surely I need not idly tolerate this fresh aggravation of my heart's grief, when learned scholars have said that kings command times and seasons. Should I not give orders to postpone the rains? And yet, the season's emblems are all that is left to do me kingly service now:

I have a regal awning bright with gold –
Lightning embroidered in the clouded sky;
Beside me stand the tossing trees, and hold

Flower-cluster fans to serve my dignity.
My court has minstrels, louder singing now
The drought is broken – peacocks prinked in blue;
And my fine citizens, the mountains, bow,
Eager to bring their streams as tribute due.

So. Does it help, then, to praise my own proper retinue? Come, I must search the woods for my beloved. [*Pause. Turning.*] I bend my will to the task, and at once here is a sight to inflame:

Those red-flushed flower-bud cups where water lies
Show me vexation's tears within her eyes.

Suppose my queen started from here, then: how shall I seek her further?

If with her gentle feet she touched the ground
Here, on a rain-wet sandy forest track,
Surely her graceful footprints can be found,
By swaying gait heel-pressed, smeared red with lac.

[*He takes a few steps, and catches sight of something.*] Here is surely a clue to tell me the way she took, in her impatient jealousy.

Marked with the tear-drops flowing,
Tinct by her sweet lips' red,
Loosed from her breast, unknowing,
There, where she stumbling fled,
There is the jade-green scarf she shed.

[*He goes forward to investigate.*] Ladybirds. And a patch of fresh grass. The woods are desolate, who will tell me of my beloved? There, on top of that massive rock which breathes out steam after the rain-storm,

A peacock perches,
While east-wind gusts ruff every tail-fan feather,
And stretches
His shriek-filled throat, eyeing the rain-cloud weather.

[*He goes up to it.*] I can at least ask.

In this wild woodland, bird of lovely blue,
  Saw you my wife whose love is true?
How could your white-flecked eyes have failed to mark
  A face so fair, slant-eyes so dark?

No reply. But the bird begins to dance. Has something pleased him, then? [*He pauses to consider.*] Yes, I understand.

  Now that my love's no longer here,
The peacock's rich paint-decorated tail,
Stirred by the wind's breath, need no rival fear.
  If she still lived, could such prevail?
When we embraced, lustres beyond compare
Shone from her flower-bedecked and tumbling hair.

No, it is useless to ask him, when he finds satisfaction in another's hurt. [*He walks on a few steps.*] There, on a rose-apple tree branch, is a hen-cuckoo: love is enkindled in her, as the fire of summer dies down. Such birds are among the wise. I shall enquire of hér, then.

Love's envoy, ever bearing lovers' greeting,
Peerless to wake a cold maid's heart to fire,
Or fetch me now my gentle one, my sweeting,
Or bring me where she rests, my heart's desire.

But, you say, how did she come to desert one who loves her so? I shall tell you:

Jealous she was,   though I gave never cause:
Not one unfaithful thought can I recall.
For womankind   need no occasion find:
The man who loves is still her willing thrall.

Ah, the bird breaks off our conversation; she is engrossed in her own thoughts:

So true it is that one man's burning pain
Ever meets cool indifference.
My earnest pleading is not even heard.
Even as I speak, she turns away,
And blind with her own passion starts to bite
A nearly ripe rose-apple fruit,
Entranced, as though she kissed a lover's lip.

Even so, I cannot be angry: her mellifluent voice awakens memories of my dear one. Let us hence. [*He begins to walk on, but almost at once stops short and listens.*] Over there, on the right! The sound of her anklets to tell me where she is walking. Now I know which way to go. [*After a step or two.*] No, no, I am deceived,

No anklets jangle. Only wild geese crying
Beneath black thunder-skies of summer's dying,
North to their loved lake-home soon to be flying.

Then I must ask these birds for news of my darling, before they lift from the water, homesick for Mānasa. [*He approaches.*] Ho, there, king of the water-birds,

Do not depart! Lake Mānasa will wait.
Leave lotus-stalks, your journey-food, awhile.
Only have pity, tell me my love's fate.
Does Virtue seek its own, that Need should court denial?

His goose-head rises, and looks, as if to say, 'My thoughts are all on Mānasa: I did not see her'.

But again, if my love you failed to see
As she passed here, frowning, close to this place,
Can you then – thief! – can you explain to me
How you know thus well to reflect her grace?

Well then, my goose,

Now you must give me back my dear:
Her graceful walk, at least, you stole.
Who's caught with part – the law is clear –
Must restitution make of all.

[*With laughter.*] Ha, there he flies! He's afraid! He knows I'm a king, with power to punish thieves. [*He continues to walk.*] And now here is a wheel-drake with his mate. And again I ask:

Wheel-bird, good-day. My love is lost . . . is fled . . .
Fine chariot-wheels I have to call my own:
But yearning thoughts all wheeling round my head
See her wheel-rounded loveliness alone.

His only answer is, 'Wha', wha'!' I can't believe it. Does he really not know who I am?

Grandchild of Sun and Moon am I by birth,
But chosen as lord by Urvashī and Earth.

Now he stays silent. In that case, I know what will catch him on the raw:

Yes, you're a splendid drake!
When a lotus-leaf in the lake
Conceals your duck, you screech with a frantic noise,
Out of your mind with fear,
When all the time she is near.
But a real grief such as mine you can still despise.

Here and in every way the adverse wind of destiny, set implacably against me, displays its power. Let me move on and explore any further possibility. [*He stops in mid-stride.*] No, not yet:

This lotus tells me, wait awhile,
And hear the humming ardent bee.
Thus her fair petal face would smile,
Would murmuring sigh when kissing me.

Most humbly I must enquire of this honey-bee, so intent on its lotus-flower. Otherwise, if I go now, I may regret it.

Tell, honeyer sweet, has she been seen by you?
[*After a moment's thought.*]
Her eyes like wine, her petal-satin brow,
Breath of her fragrant lips you never knew:
Else would all flowers be drab and scentless now.

So, we'll be on our way. [*He continues to walk, observing.*] Over there stands a majestic bull-elephant. His trunk rests on a stout branch, and his consort is by his side. From him I shall learn what has happened to my best-beloved. Gently, though: don't rush matters.

First let him relish the shoots fresh-sprung,
Wine-spiced with sap, foliage-truss
Trunk-wrenched by his mate for
Her own lord, bunched and fetched.

[*He stands still for a moment.*] He has quietly completed his breakfast, and I can ask now.

Elephant male! Herd's lord of greatest might!
My lady, slenderly superb, so fair,
  Young, with flower-dappled hair –
(The crescent moon with her would ill compare) –
Ah, does she stand in your vast range of sight?

[*Pleased.*] This rumbling deep-throated grunting is encouraging. You must mean to convey to me that you have noticed her. And we have so much in common, you and I: how can I fail to feel a kindly affection towards you?

Princes obey me: lordly beasts approve
Your kingly rule. And, as your rut still flows,
I distil bounty. Urvashī I love,

Fairest of women: so, your dear wife knows
No lord but you. – May Fortune yet avert
Loss to equate in you my tortured hurt.

Sir, my best wishes. Farewell. Onward, then, once more. [*He turns to one side, and looks off, gazing into the distance.*] Ah! – that enchanted mountain I see: the Mount of Incense, where heavenly nymphs love to sojourn. Might my pretty one be found there, on the steep flanks of the mountain? [*As he walks towards the mountain, he looks up.*] How all occasions turn against me! For my sins, even the clouds now deny me their lightning-bolts to show me the path. Even so, I shall not turn back before I have put my question.

Mountain! O tell me where my lady hides!
In deep ravine-cleft? On your sloping sides?
Or dwells my love where Love's own god resides,
Within your forests? Or perchance she rests
Her curvèd form on your round, shelving breasts?

Silence, only silence. But perhaps the mountain-peak is too far away, could not hear me. I must get closer, and ask aloud. [*He approaches.*] Mountain, tell me whether

That lost, all-lovely queen
In the fresh woodlands has been seen
There – for your majesty uplifted, high
  Soars to the gate of heaven.

[*A voice offstage, as if from the distance*]*:*

That lost, all-lovely queen
In the fresh woodlands has been seen:
Therefore Your Majesty, uplifted high,
  Soars to the gate of Heaven.

[*The King listens. With joy.*] She has been seen! The mountain heard me, quotes my own words! Have you something still more welcome to tell me? Listen, mountain, listen to me:

where is she? [*He waits, and again, from offstage, hears his own words repeated.*] Ah, heaven! Echo, only echo: my own voice rebounding from a cliff, a cave-mouth. [*His demeanour shows his despair.*] I am tired. I shall rest here, beside this mountain-stream, and find refreshment from the breeze riffling the water. The spate-waters swirl restlessly, turbid after the recent rain, and yet the sight strangely soothes my spirits.

The rippling waters – her frown-rippled brow;
There, strung-out chattering birds – her girdle-string;
Clutching the slipping, streaking foam – her dress
Loosed as she fled in passion – even now
Stumbling on stones. Is this her loveliness
Bewitched to water, still unpardoning?

I must entreat her.

Ever for you is my love, ever constant, kind,
Never unfaithful: a heart ever true I gave.
Tell me, my darling – forgiveness I pray to find –
Where is the fault that you found in your humble slave?

Or is this in very truth only a real mountain-stream? I cannot credit it that Urvashī would pass by her husband, and haste onward to unite with the ocean. So then: love's blessings are not won by sitting still, in a religious trance. I must go back to the same spot where the fair vision of her face vanished from my sight. [*After walking some distance, he stops to look.*] Ah, have I found a pointer to her path?

Here is that same Kadamba-tree: from this
  She plucked one red
Late blossom, imperfect at the summer's end,
  To adorn her head.

Here now is a stag sitting. To him I shall prefer my plea for news of my beloved.

His coat is shadow-flecked with dark –
As if the wood's presiding Shade
Cast a shy fleeting glance, to mark
The beauty of the dappled glade.

But why does he turn his head away, as if he despised me? [*Continuing to observe.*]

Towards him comes the doe,
  Slowed by her suckling fawn.
With neck bowed, he watches:
  His gaze is all for her.

Ho, stag, lord of the herd!

Have you seen my love walking within the woods?
Listen, and I shall tell how you would know her:
She has gentle eyes like those of your own companion,
Opening as wide with a look to melt the heart.

He does not heed my words, but remains as before, looking towards his wife. Well, it is understandable. The man whom Fate casts down is an object of contempt. Let us away from here. [*After some steps, he pauses and looks.*] What do I see here, burning deep red in a rock-fissure?

A blood-drop, where a lion's kill has bled?
A glowing ember? How, unquenched by rain?
[*He examines it more closely.*]
A gem refulgent! – whose Ashóka-red
The sun's dawn-fingers fumble for, in vain.

How beautiful it is! I must take it. [*Hesitating.*] But for what?

Her hair, sweet-scented from the flowers she wears,
Should by this gem most fittingly be crowned.
Never will she be found.
Why should I mist its lustre with my tears?

A VOICE [*offstage*]: Pick it up, my son, pick it up.

The goddess Pārvatī has here encrystalled
The red lac-paint of her own feet:
There is such virtue in this warm red flame
That he, who bears the same,
Must soon his own dear loved one meet.

KING [*listening*]: Who gives me this advice? [*Looks all around.*] It is a hermit, a man of great holiness, solitary in the wilds; and he has shown compassion towards me. Sir, most venerable, I humbly thank you for your most gracious words. [*He picks up the stone.*] Ah, jewel of union,

If to my empty heart she is restored,
My lost one, exquisite in grace,
I shall accord you the most honoured place
For ever in my crown:
As the young crescent moon
Adorns the head of Pārvatī's great Lord.

[*He walks on.*] Ah! [*Catching his breath.*] Why does my heart flood with tenderness? It is only a creeper, without even blossoms. And yet . . . not for nothing is it lovely to me:

A slender plant, curved shoots all wet with rain,
Like her lips washed with tears;
Void of all ornament – this is no season
Now, to put on fresh flowers;
Like her, still brooding, ever rapt in silence,
Reft of the noise of bees:
Even thus she, who in jealous rage then spurned me,
Now in remorse may mourn.

3

From KĀLIDĀSA'S *KUMĀRA-SAMBHAVA*

If the title of the poem is his – and there is no reason to doubt it – Kālidāsa intended in this work to describe the events leading up to the birth of Kumāra (also called Kārttikeya, and Skanda), the son of Shiva and the god of war in the Hindu pantheon, born to bring about the defeat of the demon Tāraka. It would seem that the poet's intention was not realized: for although the work in some of the manuscripts is in seventeen cantos, and indeed goes far beyond the birth, carrying the matter as far as the slaying of Tāraka, it is generally agreed that the later cantos are spurious, and that the genuine work of Kālidāsa goes no further than the eighth canto, thus stopping short of the actual birth.

The gods have realized that the only hope against Tāraka is a general who shall be born as the son of Shiva and Umā (Pārvatī). But Shiva has no thoughts of marriage, and is engaged in profound meditation in the remote mountain forest of the Himālaya. The third canto opens with Indra, who has come from the council of the gods, seeking the help of Kāma, the god of love, whose task it now is to cause Shiva to fall in love with Umā. Taking with him his wife Rati, and Spring as his companion, Kāma makes his way to the mountain hermitage of Shiva. Then follows a description of the coming of spring to the forest. In the presence of Umā, the god of love stretches his bow to shoot at Shiva; but at the last moment the great god catches sight of him, and in anger reduces him to ashes with a glance of fire from his third eye. (It is this catastrophe which is held to account for the epithet *ananga* 'bodiless', frequently used of the god of love.) The first attempt on Shiva, therefore, has ended in failure.

The following is a translation of the description of the coming of Spring in this canto (iii, 24–43).

And then within these mountain-forest reaches,
Skilled to distract saints' thoughts from heaven above
The young awakening Spring now yawns and stretches,
Belov'd companion of the god of love.

While the hot sun, untimely, came to waken
The North to be his love, the gentle South
Exhaled a sigh, thus to have been forsaken,
A breath warm-scented from her fragrant mouth.

The Ashóka then, its trunk and branches laden,
Full-flowered, with foil of many a green leaf-shoot,
Impatient, quite forgot to expect a maiden
To wake its flowers with anklet-tinkling foot.

On every blossom-arrow he created,
Feathered with leaves and tipped with mango-flame,
The fletcher Spring the owner designated,
Writing with bees the god of love's own name.

The Karnikāra's blossom, brightly glowing,
While by its scentlessness it grieved the mind,
Showed how God's will is set against bestowing
All excellences in one place combined.

Curved like the crescent moon, deep crimson traces
Glowed as Palāsha-buds began to swell,
As if the nail-marks of the Spring's embraces
Flushed on the forest-lands he loved so well.

Spring's Loveliness, with woman's wiles acquainted,
With flowers of Tilaka[1] adorned her head,
Made beauty-spots of clinging bees, and painted
Fresh mango-blossom lips with morning-red.

1. The word *tilaka*, besides being the name of a flowering shrub, also denotes an ornamental (or sectarian) mark painted on the forehead.

Piyāla-blossom clusters shed their pollen
In smoke-clouds; and the deer, bewildered, blind,
Through forest-glades where rustling leaves had fallen,
Made rash by springtime, coursed against the wind.

The cuckoo's song, hoarsened to gentle cooing,
When food of mango-sprouts tightened his throat,
Became the voice of Love, to work the undoing
Of maids cold-hearted, by its magic note.

The fairy-women, with their winter faces
Devoid of lipstick, saw their colour fade,
While with the Spring the rising sweat left traces,
Smearing the beauty-marks so carefully made.

When, in the forest of their meditation,
The holy hermits saw the untimely spring,
Their minds were hard-pressed to resist temptation,
To keep their thoughts from Love's imagining.

When Love came there, his flower-bow ready stringing,
With fair Desire, his consort, at his side,
The forest creatures showed the passion springing
In every bridegroom's heart towards his bride.

From the same flower-cup which his love had savoured
The black bee sipped the nectar as a kiss;
While the black doe, by her own consort favoured,
Scratched by his antlers, closed her eyes in bliss.

The elephant with water lotus-scented
Sprayed her own lord, giving of love a token;
The wheel-drake, honouring his wife, presented
A half-chewed lotus-stalk which he had broken.

When nectar-wine had set her eyes a-dancing,
And sweat had smudged the fairy's painted face,
Her fairy-lover found her more entrancing,
And checked his song to seek a fresh embrace.

When trembling petal-lips made laughing faces,
And blossom-breasts the slender stems were bending,
Even the forest-trees received the embraces
Of creeper-wives, from their bough-arms depending.

Yet Shiva still remained in meditation
Absorbed, although he heard the singing elves:
Can anything have power of perturbation
Of souls completely masters of themselves?

Then at the doorway of his forest dwelling
With rod of gold his servant Nandi stood,
Frowning, with finger to his lips, thus quelling
The unseemly conduct in the springtime wood.

Throughout the forest, at his simple stricture,
Dumb were the birds, and silent were the bees:
As in a scene fixed in a painted picture,
Stilled were the deer and motionless the trees.

As on a journey under baleful omen,
Trying in fear from Shiva's eyes to hide,
To the Lord's sacred ground came Love the bowman,
Entering through creeper-thickets from the side.

4

Invocation

Loving the manly virtues, they delight
To point his faults out in the plainest way;
They'll give their souls to him they love, despite
The fact their eyes will ne'er their hearts betray.
When they most long for love, their affirmation
Is constantly expressed as firm negation.
May Women smile on you: the most perverse,
Delightful creatures in God's universe.

160

'Dear child . . .' – 'My lord . . .' – 'Do not be angry.' – 'Why,
What makes you think I am?' – 'Forgive me' – 'You?
You have done nothing wrong: the faults all lie
With me.' – 'Then why those tears, the sobs you try
To stifle?' – 'Who's to see?' – 'Myself.' – 'And who
Am I?' – 'My love.' – 'Ah no. And so I cry.'

Amaru

161

'Leave me alone', I said,
– Only in fun, you understand – and then
He simply rose at once, and left my bed.
What can one do with men?
Oh! he is heartless, pitiless, although
I shamelessly desire
His love's false-promised fire.
Dear sister! What, o what am I to do?

Amaru

162

When his mouth faced my mouth, I turned aside
And steadfastly gazed only at the ground;
I stopped my ears, when at each coaxing word
They tingled more; I used both hands to hide
My blushing, sweating cheeks. Indeed I tried.
But oh, what could I do, then, when I found
My bodice splitting of its own accord?

Amaru

163

A chance swift glance;
Her eyebrow bow with casual cunning bended;
Words' witching spell;
Laughter, fading in maiden modesty;
Unstudied stance;
Cool graceful steps wherein love's fire is blended:
Woman knows well
These are her ornaments, her armoury.

Bhartṛhari

164

No more evasions, please. Consider well
The facts, and tell where best to seek for rest:
At court, or exiled where flanked mountains swell?
Or in her smile, reclining on her breast?

Bhartṛhari

165

If a professor thinks what matters most
Is to have gained an academic post
Where he can earn a livelihood, and then
Neglect research, let controversy rest,
He's but a petty tradesman at the best,
Selling retail the work of other men.

Kālidāsa

166

In this vain world, when men of intellect
Must soil their souls with service, to expect
A morsel at a worthless prince's gate,
How could they ever hope to renovate
Their spirits? – were it not that fate supplies
The swinging girdles and the lotus eyes –
Women, with swelling breasts that comfort soon,
Wearing the beauty of the rising moon.

Bhartṛhari

167

In this vain fleeting universe, a man
Of wisdom has two courses: first, he can
Direct his time to pray, to save his soul,
And wallow in religion's nectar-bowl;
But, if he cannot, it is surely best
To touch and hold a lovely woman's breast,
And to caress her warm round hips, and thighs,
And to possess that which between them lies.

Bhartṛhari

168

'No! don't!' she says at first, while she despises
The very thought of love; then she reveals
A small desire; and passion soon arises,
Shyly at first, but in the end she yields.
With confidence then playing without measure
Love's secret game, at last no more afraid
She spreads her legs wide in her boundless pleasure.
Ah! love is lovely with a lovely maid!

Bhartṛhari

169

Loosed are the vows of love we used to make,
His heart's esteem has melted all away,
A common man, heedless of constancy.
How can I help but in imagination
Picture these thoughts, as day succeeds to day,
Dear sister mine? Why, in my desolation,
Why does my heart not break?

Amaru

170

'Go if you must,' she said, 'and I shall pray
That Heaven may guard you on your way;
And I shall be reborn again, I swear,
Wherever you may be, my dear.'

Daṇḍin

171

It is small wonder that my lady's breasts
Rise firm and proud –
For who would not be proud to be
Close to her heart?

172

Close in the tight embrace her breasts were pressed,
Her skin thrilled; and between her pretty thighs
The oil-smooth sap of love has overflowed.
'No, not again, my darling. Let me rest;
Don't make me . . .', whispering, pleading soft, she sighs.
Is she asleep? or dying? or else melted
Into my heart? Or is she but a dream?

Amaru

173

'Yes, you are fawning at my feet,' said she,
'A wretched trick,' she said, 'to hide your chest
Smeared with the evidence – in case I see
Cosmetics from another woman's breast.'
'Where is it, then?' I said, and with a kiss
Pressed close to her, to blur the tell-tale trace,
Holding her firm, arousing her to bliss. –
And she forgot it in our fierce embrace.

Amaru

174

Her thighs – so firm they are, and round,
And so extremely smooth withal,
That nowhere in the world at all
Can fitting similes be found.

175

To her waist

This is sheer recklessness! How can she make you
Go for a walk?
Can she not see that the weight of her breasts
Is enough to break you?

176

Fluttering her hands, she tries to find her clothes,
And throws her broken garland at the lamp,
Laughing in shy confusion, while she tries
To cover up my eyes. How sweet she is
To look and look at, after we've made love!

Amaru

177

Nectar is nectar: there is no dispute;
Honey still honey-sweet; the mango-fruit
Filled with sweet juice. – But you, who know so well,
You connoisseurs of tasting, come now, tell
Impartially, discarding fear and favour,
What sweet is sweet beside her sweet lips' savour?

178

The impercipient may compare
A lady to a leech;
But this is wrong: a lady fair
– As little thought will teach –
Is not the same. A leech takes blood
And nothing else at all
From wretched men: but she takes food,
And mind, and strength, and soul.

179

Nor gifts, nor honour, righteousness nor praise,
Learning nor force, can mend a woman's ways.

180

Dear Lotus-eyes, if in your heart alone
Anger now reigns, a lover, to enslave you,
What can I do? – But give me back my own,
The kisses, the embraces I once gave you.

Amaru

181

The god of love can scarce be matched
In skill in shooting with his arrow:
My body is not even scratched,
And yet he's pierced me to the marrow!

182

I burn with anguish when we are apart,
When he returns, with jealous fear;
And when I see him, he assaults my heart;
I faint when he is near.
No single moment can I capture bliss,
When he is gone, or when he's here.
What in this world can be more strange than this?
And yet, he is my dear.

Amaru

183

'Look, darling, how we've disarranged the bed:
Now it's too hard with rubbed-off sandal-paste,
Too rough for your soft skin,' he said,
'Come, lie on me instead.'
While he distracted me with kisses sweet,
All of a sudden, with his feet
In pincer-fashion then he caught
My sari firmly by the hem:
And so the sly rogue forced me then
To move the way he ought.

Amaru

184

They are firm, and you are tender,
Full and round, though you are slender:
Bold your breasts, while you are shy
– Since so near your heart they lie.

185

It is the jewels that are bedecked by women,
Not women who are beautified by them:
A woman unbejewelled will still enrapture,
But who looks twice at any girl-less gem?

186

Oh, it was careless when her Maker
Made her a waist so slender!
Suppose a breath of wind should break her:
How would he ever mend her?

187

Let fools then quarrel, or in slumber laze:
Music and learning fill the wise man's days.

188

Burning from Shiva's wrath, the god of love
Plunged in the lake between my lady's thighs
To quench the flames; and hence as smoke arise
The curling hairs on Venus' mount above.

189

Love all you can,
Handsome young man.
Day after day
Youth steals away.
While you still live,
Why should you give
Death, for his share,
Something so fair?

190

Her eager lover still she tried to keep
From intercourse, the longer to enjoy
Love's tender talk; and the impassioned boy
Quite suddenly fell fast asleep.

191

Soft as a bud her betel-scarlet lips,
Skin stained with sandal-paste, and brimming eyes
Running eye-shadow as the fountain sprays;
Damp hair, flower-scented, dripping dress that grips
And shows her body all. – What charms arise
From Beauty bathing late on summer days!

192

Let my sole view be of my love:
For which religious views in fashion
Could win such bliss of heaven above? –
And that, without discarding passion.

193

Surely the god of love became her willing slave,
Obedient to the orders that her glances gave.

Bhartṛhari

194

A lover reunited with his darling,
The bee clings close and kisses the mango-blossom.

195

Her heart as hard to hold as mirrored face;
Like mountain-tracks, her inclination weaves,
Narrow, rough, twisting, difficult to find;
Like water drops on lotus-leaf her mind.
Wise men proclaim it: woman grows apace
Her armour, like a creeper's poison leaves.

196

My clever skin!
When the cold wind blows,
And I'm short of clothes,
How well it knows
How to wrap me in,
When the goose-skin grows.

197

To quarrel with them is a loss of face;
To have their friendship is a sad disgrace:
A man of sterling judgement realizes
What fools are worth, and foolish men despises.

Bhāravi

198

My love and I play dice: the prize
(Which one must lose) is that which lies
  Between her thighs.
But, either way, let Love proclaim,
Which of us two has won the game?

199

The cage of this poor frame would surely burst apart,
But for the cords of fancy fashioned by my heart.

200

When I was with her, her glance was still circumspect,
Though she would smile when I spoke of external things;
Modest her bearing: her love was not yet revealed,
  Nor was it quite concealed.

Kālidāsa

201

Is she a pencil of ambrosia?
Is she a swelling flood of loveliness?
Is she the beauty of the lotus flower?
Is she a budding, flowering vine of love?
Now that I've seen this lovely, charming girl,
I cannot help but think that all the world,
Except for her, is utterly in vain.

202

Winter

Both hands clenched,
Running eyes and nose
And shivering skin:
As if in a painting,
The traveller stands on the river-bank
Despairing how to get across.

203

He marvelled at her breasts, and when he'd seen them
He shook his head, to disengage his gaze
Trapped in between them.

204

If you intend to show a face
Empty of feeling, whence this look of fire?
If it is silence you desire,
Whence is this trembling of your lips' sweet grace?
If you would force your eyes to meditation,
Why does your body thrill with bliss?
Dearest, forget this feigned exasperation,
And end it with a kiss.

Amaru

205

I am here and I am thine,
Thou art there and thou art mine:
Intercourse of minds is best,
Dearest one. Who wants the rest?

206

Sweet, be not proud to tell yourself that he
Has painted on your cheek some ornaments:
He'd do the same for any other she –
Save that the trembling of his hand prevents.

207

Such bitter grief as this has cracked my heart,
Which still has not burst apart;
And from my body, fainting from the smart,
The senses do not depart.
Internal fires within my body blaze,
And yet I am not consumed:
Fortune has cleft me with a mortal wound,
Yet still I live out my days.

Bhavabhūti

208

When he desired to see her breast
She clasped him tight in an embrace;
And when he wished to kiss her lip
She used cosmetics on her face.
She held his hand quite firmly pressed
Between her thighs in desperate grip;
Nor yielded yet to his caress,
Yet kept alive his wantonness.

209

I've gazed upon the river's waves, and seen
A bunch of water-weed, and shining pearls
All set in gems. But now the moon is cleansed
Of all her stains; and still the lotus blooms
Unsleeping; and a loving pair of birds
Are nestling close. And who has seen the like?

210

Your breasts are like two kings at war, my dear:
Each striving to invade the other's sphere.

211

When he had filled her with the joy of love,
He tried to pull aside her slipping dress
So as to gaze upon her loveliness:
But still her girdle shone with gems above,
And so he did not quite succeed to see,
Nor could she modestly retreat: her lover
Failed to unveil her nakedness, while she,
No more successful, strove herself to cover.

212

Still in the hamlets of this wretched land
Some families exist, though thinned and torn
By harsh oppression of a landlord's hand,
Yet loath to leave the homes where they were born.
And now the mongoose wanders where he will
Where only broken thatch and walls remain;
From their pale, liquid throats, the pigeons still
Murmur with beauty, to assuage the pain.

213

I never earned me any wealth,
  Nor managed scholarship to gain,
Nor did a thing for my soul's health:
  My life has slipped away in vain.

214

Here, forest-fires; there, tangled thickets; and
The dogged hunter stalks, and bends his bow;
In front, a python: dropped by Heaven's hand,
What can the fawn now do? Where can he go?

215

I left a loving new-wed wife behind,
And slaved at books, and slept upon the ground,
And lived on alms, and disciplined my mind,
To win the wisdom waiting to be found.
Yet, with the ages' knowledge I inherit,
Throughout the land no patronage I find.
Why should a man for learning vex his spirit,
Gaining nor comfort nor religious merit?

216

With tail-fans spread, and undulating wings
With whose vibrating pulse the air now sings,
Their voices lifted and their beaks stretched wide,
Treading the rhythmic dance from side to side,
Eying the raincloud's dark, majestic hue,
Richer in colour than their own throats' blue,
With necks upraised, to which their tails advance,
Now in the rains the screaming peacocks dance.

217

The spring has lengthened out its days
With fragments of cold winter's night;
The pregnant flame-flower still delays
To warm the world with blossom bright;
And now the sun and shadow meet
An equal shade to equal height:
And still we lack the warmth to greet
The coming of the spring's delight.

218

Look at the cloud-cat, lapping there on high
With lightning tongue the moon-milk from the sky!

Yogeśvara

219

These wooden-hearted critics, how can they
Know anything of poets' poetry
Fresh as a fragrant jasmine bud? But come,
Forget this nonsense, hearken to my rune:
For poetry's moonray nectar melts a stone.

220

Sweet girl, your dress has come apart
While you lie in the heather;
And here am I, with lonely heart:
Why don't we sleep together?

221

When trod upon or struck, a snake will slay.
But slanderous men
Are something else again,
Whispering in B's ear, and destroying A.

222

See, the arched back, the tail erected, stiff,
Bent at the tip and twisting, and the ear
Flat to the head, and the eye quick with fear
Darting a single glance, debating if
The way to get inside the house is clear:
And on the other side, its gullet fat
With panting, growling, hoarse with its own breath,
With sneering lips that lift to show his teeth,
And slavering jaws, the dog attacks the cat.

Yogeśvara

223

'She is lovely' – 'She is tender' –
'And her waist, it is so slender' –
'She is sweet' – 'Her modest glances' –
'And my heart she quite entrances':
All the time when you're away,
Sings my soul this litany.

224

The lamps were lit and the night far spent,
And he, my love, was on love intent
– And he knew full well just what loving meant:
But he made his love in a cautious way,
For the wretched bed upon which we lay
Creaked, and had far too much to say.

225

Is it a miracle? Or does my mind
Betray me, that the moon has left the skies?
Yet wonder upon wonder here I find:
Twin lotus-blossoms, opening their eyes.

226

I rolled them in turmeric, cummin, and spice,
With masses of pepper to make them taste nice:
In lashings of sesamum oil I then fried 'em –
The pungency curled up my tongue when I tried 'em:
I neglected to wash, and got down to the dish,
And I swallowed that curry of nice little fish.

227

A day he does no harm, an evil man
Counts as a *dies non* in his life's span.

228

Soft breeze, sweet perfumed with the fragrant scent
Of jasmine white and gold, caress her face,
Brush with your breath her breast and bring content,
The scented fragrance of her sweet embrace.

Bhavabhūti

229

When we have loved, my love,
Panting and pale from love,
Then from your cheeks, my love,
Scent of the sweat I love:
And when our bodies love
Now to relax in love
After the stress of love,
Ever still more I love
Our mingled breath of love.

230

Mere lotuses I can no longer prize;
The sweetest honey I must criticize;
I laugh at nectar's sweetness – what is this?
For I have drunk a stronger draught of bliss:
The deadly glances of her loving eyes.

231

Churn water in your churn to get you butter,
And squeeze a bit of stone and hope for honey;
Or else your fevered frame perhaps you'd cool,
Washed in the waves of the mirage's pool?
Perhaps you'd rather try to get a drink
Milking that worn-out she-ass? What do you think?
It's not so foolish as to earn the money
To live upon, by service to an utter
    Knave and fool.

232

And all around the village now,
When ground is broken by the plough
The village sparrows hop and play:
Small, curved beaks pecking dusty clay;
And, while each wing the wind supplies
To raise the dust, blink beady eyes.

233

This is no place for you to spend the night.
Well, you're a stranger here – how could you know?
The master grudges every single bite,
And no-one ever comes here: not a single crow.

234

Lying together in the bed
They kept a sullen silence grim,
And not a word to her he said,
And she refused to speak to him.
But glances chance to interlace:
A moment's pause, and both thereafter
Forget resentment, and embrace
Dissolving in a gale of laughter.

Amaru

235

Earth, my own mother; father Air; and Fire,
My friend; and Water, well-beloved cousin;
And Ether, brother mine: to all of you
This is my last farewell. I give you thanks
For all the benefits you have conferred
During my sojourn with you. Now my soul
Has won clear, certain knowledge, and returns
To the great Absolute from whence it came.

Bhartṛhari

236

Pronounce in universals; and my mind
  Presents only particulars to me:
Speak the word 'Woman', and at once I find
  In my mind's eye one woman fair I see.

237

We'll even fear our next-of-kin,
When harmed by strangers' deeds or words:
Once scalded by hot milk, the child
Will even blow to cool his curds.

238

Aroused at last with laughter to the height
Of love's abandon, she fought hard to gain
The victory of love, with all her might:
But when her slender frame had still not quite
Achieved her aim, she realized at length
The undertaking was beyond her strength;
And, out of breath, before she won the prize,
She lay quite still, and her shy, rueful eyes
Pleaded with mine, that I should end the game.

239

The heron seeking supper in the lake
Darts his sharp eye around; his careful feet
Move gently, gently, every step they take.
Now with one leg withdrawn into the air
He twists his neck awry to spy his prey,
Alert for every moving lotus-leaf,
In case it should turn out to be a fish.

240

On the sacred cow

Unfit to bear a burden,
Unskilled to pull a plough,
These temple-courtyard oxen:
But one thing, you'll allow –
They're pretty good at eating.

241

With tumbled hair of swarms of bees,
And flower-robes dancing in the breeze,
With sweet, unsteady lotus-glances,
Intoxicated, Spring advances.

242

Sometimes he tries to open wide his eyes,
Rubs with his hand, and screws them up to peer,
Holds at a distance, and again he tries
To see if it looks any clearer near,
Takes it at last outside, in case the bright
Sunlight might help, to see how it will look,
Wondering if ointment would improve his sight
– The aged scholar trying to read a book.

243

First find yourself a charming girl,
And while she says, 'No, no!'
And while with trembling voice she cries,
'You scoundrel, let me go!'
And while with rage her eyebrows dance,
And while she squirms and hisses,
Just go ahead and use your strength,
And steal yourself some kisses.
Then you will find that this is how
Mere mortal men obtain
Ambrosia, while the foolish gods
Once churned the sea in vain.

Amaru

244

Hand in clasped hand and side pressed close to side,
Silently stand some children of the poor,
And shyly, hungry eyes half-turned aside,
Observe the eater through the open door.

245

Her lovesome, tripping walk; her glances bright,
From downcast eyes; the gentle words she said:
The god of love united them, and made
A weapon irresistible in might.

246

A panicle of flowers on love's own tree,
A pledge of nectar stored in joy's own vault,
Shaped by skilled hands of Fortune, without fault,
A honey-salve to soothe the world's tired eyes;
Of Love's fair land, the charming river she,
Where waterfalls of loveliness cascade:
Who will be worthy of this gentle maid,
The shore to which her beauty's waves might rise?

247

If he had seen this dainty creature,
Golden as saffron in every feature,
How could a high creator bear
To part with anything so fair?
Suppose he shut his eyes? Oh, no:
How could he then have made her so?
– Which proves the universe was not created:
Buddhist theology is vindicated.

Dharmakīrti

248

Her hand upon her hip she placed,
And swayed seductively her waist;
With chin upon her shoulder pressed,
She stretched herself to show her breast:
With sapphire pupils burning bright
Within the pearly orbs of white,
Her eyes with eagerness did dance,
And threw me a come-hither glance.

249

I'm a footless traveller, very well read,
And yet no scholar (I've got no head);
Without any mouth, speaking truth or lies.
– Riddle me this, and you'll be wise.

250

When in love's fight they came to grips,
'Neath wounds of teeth and nails she sank;
And might have died – save that she drank
Ambrosia from her lover's lips.

251

This life on earth 's a poison tree,
And yet with two fruits sweet:
Ambrosia of poesy,
And joy when true friends meet.

252

Her red Ashóka-flowers chid the ruby's brightness,
While Karnikāras stole the flame-gold of morning;
Pearls paled beside her Sinduvāra's whiteness:
Such flowers of spring she wore for her adorning.

Kālidāsa

253

Untimely, cut by Fate:
But in the hearts of friends
Memories,
Like a great bell, reverberate.

254

Look, Love: the flag of victory –
A grey hair plain to view!
Your futile darts are naught to me.
Now, I shall conquer you.

Dharmakīrti

255

'Did you sleep in the garden, dear,
On a bed of magnolia flowers?
I suppose you know that your breast
Is smeared with the pollen dust?'
'O, why will you try to be clever,
And scold me with hints like this?
Let me tell you I got these scratches
From cruel magnolia thorns.'

256

Though she's the girl, I am the one who's shy;
And though she walks with heavy hips, it's I
Who cannot move for heaviness; and she
Who is the woman: but the coward, me.
She is the one with high and swelling breast,
But I the one with weariness oppressed.
Clearly, in her the causal factors lie,
But the effects in me. I wonder why!

Amaru
(*also ascribed to Dharmakīrti*)

257

For one short act, a child; next act, a boy
In love; then poor; a short act to enjoy
Status and wealth: till in the last act, Man,
Painted with wrinkles, body bent with age,
Ending the comedy which birth began,
Withdraws behind the curtain of life's stage.

Bhartṛhari

258

Last night in private, while the household slept,
With passion unrestrained, Love's feast they kept:
And when, this morning, at the breakfast table,
Their glances meet in joy, they do their best
To guard their secret from the older people,
And hide the merry laughter in their breast.

Amaru

259

Harder than diamond? Softer than a flower?
    Well,
    Who can tell
The minds of men held in religion's power,
    Or spell?

Bhavabhūti

260

Her breasts are high,
Her waist lies low;
And next, an upthrust hip:
If on uneven ground you go –
Why, any man might trip.

261

The stake we played for, noose of love's embrace,
After love's fire the fan to cool my face:
Alas, when I am now by Fate bereft,
This scarf of hers is all that I have left.

262

The tender words she spoke so sweet
Last night when in his arms she lay,
She hears the parrot now repeat,
And blushes at the break of day.

263

He leaves the nest;
And flaps his wings;
And stops, and struts;
And bit by bit,
He makes his way
To top of tree:
A n d,
His neck up,
His tail up,
His foot up,
His comb up,
The cock lifts
His voice up,
And
C r o w s.

vidyābhilāṣakupitāṃ nijabālasakhyā
tandryā kathaṃcid anunīya samīpanītām
cetoharāṃ praṇayinīm akhilendriyeṣṭāṃ
nidrām prasādayitum adya namaskaromi.

She who forsook me, when I fondly burned
The midnight oil at Fame's false shrine, has now
By her young sister Sloth – I know not how –
Been pacified, and home to me returned.
  My yearning heart, I swear, henceforth I'll keep
  Constant in worship of my first love, Sleep.

References to the Sanskrit originals

Many of the verses appear in several other anthologies; but in general no attempt has been made to go outside the sources named here. Nor did it seem necessary to attempt to be exhaustive, even within these limits.

A *Amaru-śataka*, Kāvyamālā series, 18, 2nd edition, Nirṇayasāgara Press, Bombay, 1900 (and subsequent reprints).

B Bhartṛhari: *Śatakatrayādi-subhāṣitasaṃgraha: The Epigrams attributed to Bhartṛhari*, ed. D. D. Kosambi, Bombay, 1948. (Verses numbered 1–200 are in all the major recensions, and may be considered genuine; nos. 201–352 are verses missing in one or more of the major recensions, and are of doubtful authenticity, in varying degrees, though some of them may be genuine; while numbers higher than 352, from single recensions, or attributed to Bhartṛhari in anthologies, are almost without exception to be considered as late interpolations, among which, in any case, not more than two or three are of sufficient merit to justify the attribution.)

IS *Indische Sprüche, Sanskrit und Deutsch*, herausgegeben von Otto Böhtlingk, 3 vols., 2nd edition, St Petersburg, 1870–73. (Numbers in brackets following references to this are the numbers of the same verses in the selection included by Böhtlingk in his *Sanskrit Chrestomathie*, 3rd edition, Leipzig, 1909.)

P *The Paddhati of Śārṅgadhara: a Sanskrit Anthology*, ed. Peter Peterson, Bombay Sanskrit Series, no. xxxvii, Bombay, 1888.

R *The Subhāṣitaratnakoṣa, compiled by Vidyākara*, ed. D. D. Kosambi and V. V. Gokhale, Harvard Oriental Series, vol. 42; Cambridge, Mass., 1957.

S *The Subhāshitāvali of Vallabhedeva*, ed. Peter Peterson, Bombay Sanskrit Series, no. xxxi, Bombay, 1886.

Introductory verses: *Raghuvaṃśa* i. 1–4

1 (a) *Mālavikāgnimitra*, prologue, 2

(b) *Mālatī-mādhava*, prologue, 8

2 S. 134 (cf. R. 1721)

3 S. 140, 141, 153

4 B. 200

5 S. 1190, 1191 (notes)

6 S. 1049

7 S. 1106

8 B. 91

9 B. 120

10 S. 1208

11 B. 87

12 B. 77

13 B. 108

14 B. 104

15 B. 82

16 IS. 1311 (103); P. 3634; S. 1969

17 B. 312

18 B. 81

19 IS. 1108 (87); S. 1610

20 B. 114

21 S. 757

22 S. 975

23 B. 136

24 S. 1260

25 S. 1310

26 B. 118

27 B. 121

28 B. 110

29 S. 764

30 *Śakuntalā* 55

31 *Śakuntalā* 44

32 *Śakuntalā* 20

33 *Mālatī-mādhava* i. 24; R. 446

34 R. 768

35 R. 919

36 R. 830
37 A. 31; S. 1947; P. 3613; R. 835
38 R. 454; S. 1472
39 S. 1467; P. 3268; R. 456; *Vikramorvaśīya* i. 10
40 R. 458; S. 1517; P. 3320
41 R. 459
42 R. 498; S. 1977; P. 3323
43 R. 500; S. 1254; P. 3368
44 R. 478; S. 1232; P. 3451
45 R. 477; P. 566
46 R. 501
47 B. 130; S. 1235
48 IS. 184 (17)
49 B. 169 (reading *sā ramyā nagarī*)
50 S. 690
51 IS. 167 (14)
52 S. 2938; IS. 3899 (224)
53 IS. 3915 (225)
54 IS. 3302, 3304 (216, 217)
55 IS. 536 (51)
56 IS. 2776 (200)
57 B. 153
58 IS. 1590 (118)
59 IS. 818 (69)
60 IS. 834 (70)
61 IS. 746 (63)
62 IS. 940 (80)
63 IS. 1093 (85)
64 B. 422; IS. 1190 (92); S. 3195
65 IS. 1264 (99)
66 B. 221; IS. 1460 (112); P. 465
67 R. 1494; IS. 1636 (121); P. 261
68 R. 251; S. 1765; P. 3869
69 A. 71; R. 816
70 B. 237
71 B. 32
72 S. 1529

73 B. 63; *Śakuntalā* 5. 13
74 B. 39
75 B. 58
76 B. 5; R. 1217
77 IS. 2205 (165)
78 IS. 2247 (170)
79 IS. 2347 (176); S. 1476
80 IS. 2469 (186)
81 *Mṛcchakaṭikā* 5.28; IS. 2353 (178)
82 *Böhtlingk, Sanskrit Chrestomathie*, 185
83 R. 905; S. 1994; P. 3640
84 R. 871
85 IS. 1583 (117)
86 *Böhtlingk, Sanskrit Chrestomathie*, 187
87 IS. 2664 (193)
88 IS. 2745 (198)
89 *Mṛcchakaṭikā* i. 38
90 *Uttararāma-carita* i. 38; R. 427
91 S. 151; IS. 2858 (207)
92 A. 13
93, 94 (References lost: late verses in the style of Amaru?)
95 *Böhtlingk, Sanskrit Chrestomathie*, 226; P. 671
96 P. 3356
97 B. 276; IS. 4333 (241)
98 The only Prakrit verse included in this volume. The text (quoted in *Dhvanyāloka* under i. 14) has several inaccuracies in the printed editions and should read:

cumbijjai saahuttaṃ avaruṇḍijjai sahassahuttaṃ pi
viramia puṇo ramijjai pie jaṇe ṇatthi puṇaruttaṃ.

99 S. 1044
100 P. 144
101 B. 190; IS. 4772
102 Quoted in commentary to Rudraṭa's *Kāvyālankāra*: Keith, *History of Sanskrit Literature*, p. 204; Peterson, Introduction to *Subhāṣitāvali*, p. 56.
103 IS. 7590
104 IS. 4364 (246)

105 IS. 4588 (259). (Almost the same sense, in entirely different Sanskrit words, S. 2402.)
106 *Mṛcchakaṭikā* i. 13
107 P. 818
108 R. 1329
109 B. 313; R. 1330
110 IS. 5546
111 P. 804
112 IS. 5594 (296)
113 *Böhtlingk, Sanskrit Chrestomathie*, 300
114 B. 718; P. 402
115 B. 712; S. 754
116 IS. 5920 (309)
117 B. 177; S. 3475; P. 308
118 A. 125; P. 3426; S. 1114; IS. 5968 (311)
119 P. 409; IS. 6049 (313)
120 IS. 6497 (323)
121 IS. 6588 (324)
122 B. 770; IS. 6671 (329)
123 S. 1270, 2232; IS. 5194 (280)
124 IS. 4715
125 *Ratnāvalī* 46; IS. 4686
126 B. 759; S. 2943
127 *Bāla-rāmāyaṇa* ii. 17; *Viddhaśālabhañjikā* i. 14; R. 457; P. 3373
128 B. 163; R. 1222; S. 3473; P. 204
129 B. 165
130 B. 296
131 B. 311
132 IS. 4881
133 IS. 4889
134 R. 1304
135 A. 70; IS. 4983
136 IS. 4935
137 IS. 4891
138 IS. 4956; P. 380
139 S. 1366; IS. 5050
140 IS. 5076

141 B. 171
142 A. 69
143 A. 114
144 A. 16; R. 621; S. 2214; P. 3743
145 *Anargharāghava* vii. 87; R. 443; P. 3221
146 P. 508
147 P. 498
148 P. 499
149 Keith, *History of Sanskrit Literature*, p. 209
150 S. 2141–2; cf. R. 574
151 P. 509
152 Keith, *History of Sanskrit Literature*, p. 200
153 B. 8
154 B. 319, 9
155 IS. 6615
156 IS. 6608–9
157 R. 1680
158 S. 1313
159 S. 1311
Invocation verse: R. 384; P. 3079
160 A. 57
161 A. 15
162 A. 11
163 B. 92
164 B. 84
165 *Mālavikāgnimitra* i. 17
166 B. 97
167 B. 88
168 B. 124
169 A. 43; R. 697
170 S. 1040; P. 3393; *Kāvyādarśa* ii. 141
171 S. 1536
172 A. 40
173 A. 26; S. 2109
174 S. 1564
175 S. 1549
176 A. 90; R. 591

177 IS. 532 (50)
178 IS. 2368–9
179 IS. 3283
180 A. 133
181 R. 330
182 R. 734
183 A. 74
184 P. 3339
185 P. 3086
186 S. 1551
187 P. 202
188 S. 1558
189 S. 2366
190 S. 2050
191 IS. 81
192 P. 3514
193 B. 127; R. 489
194 S. 1647; P. 3785
195 IS. 75
196 R. 1318
197 *Kirātārjunīya* xiv. 24; R. 1674; S. 436
198 S. 2048
199 R. 1319
200 *Śakuntalā* ii. 11; R. 505
201 R. 431
202 S. 1850
203 R. 438
204 A. 149; R. 638; S. 1625
205 R. 1648
206 R. 1640
207 *Uttararāma-carita* iii. 31; *Mālatī-mādhava* ix. 12; R. 755
208 R. 690
209 R. 452
210 R. 461
211 R. 559
212 R. 1175
213 R. 1512

214 R. 1508
215 R. 1478
216 R. 236
217 R. 167
218 R. 257
219 R. 1278
220 R. 822
221 R. 1268
222 R. 1163
223 R. 480
224 R. 573
225 R. 390
226 R. 1148
227 R. 1290
228 *Mālatī-mādhava*, i. 41; R. 754
229 R. 575
230 R. 530
231 R. 1515
232 R. 1162
233 R. 1328
234 A. 23; R. 667; S. 2112; P. 3715
235 B. 301
236 R. 534
237 R. 1265
238 R. 585; S. 2129
239 R. 1164
240 S. 953
241 S. 1672
242 R. 1179
243 A. 36
244 R. 1320
245 R. 386
246 R. 430
247 R. 440
248 R. 465
249 P. 514 (answer: a letter)
250 R. 586

251 IS. 6636
252 *Kumāra-sambhava* iii. 53
253 R. 1253
254 R. 1518
255 R. 632
256 A. 34; R. 481
257 B. 235
258 R. 619; S. 2212; P. 3741; A. 150
259 *Uttararāma-carita* ii. 7; R. 1244; P. 215
260 R. 379; S. 1268; P. 3370
261 R. 764
262 S. 2162
263 R. 1156
264 Attributed to Lakṣmīdāsa, author of the *Śukasaṃdeśa*.

THE PENGUIN CLASSICS

THE EPIC OF GILGAMESH

English Version by N. K. Sandars

Miraculously preserved on clay tablets which were deciphered in the last century, *The Epic of Gilgamesh* is at least 1,500 years older than Homer. This volume contains a straightforward English version of the adventures of the great King of Uruk in his fruitless search for immortality and of his friendship with Enkidu, the wild man from the hills. Also included in the epic is another legend of the Flood which agrees in many details with the Biblical story of Noah.

HOMER

THE ILIAD

Translated by E. V. Rieu

The Greeks considered the *Iliad* their greatest literary achievement. Out of a single episode in the Tale of Troy, Achilles' withdrawal from the fighting and his return to kill the Trojan hero Hector, Homer created a timeless, dramatic tragedy. His characters are heroic but their passions and problems are human and universal, and he presents them with compassion, understanding, and humour against the harsh background of war.

VIRGIL

THE AENEID

Translated by W. F. Jackson Knight

The Aeneid of Virgil (70–19 B.C.) describes the legendary origin of the Roman nation. It tells of the Trojan prince Aeneas, who escaped, with some followers, after Troy fell, and sailed to Italy. Here they settled and laid the foundations of Roman power. *The Aeneid* is a poet's picture of the world, where human affairs are controlled by human and superhuman influences. It is a great literary epic inspired by Virgil's love of his native Italy and his sense of Rome's destiny as a civilized ruler of nations.

THE PENGUIN CLASSICS

HINDU MYTHS

Translated by Wendy O'Flaherty

These tales of Hindu gods and demons express in vivid symbols the metaphysical insights of ancient Indian priests and poets. This new selection and translation of seventy-five seminal myths spans the wide range of classical Indian sources, from the serpent-slaying Indra of the Vedas (c. 1200 B.C.) to the medieval pantheon – the phallic and ascetic Śiva, the maternal and blood-thirsty Goddess, the mischievous child Krishna, the other avatars of Vishnu, and the many minor gods, demons, rivers and animals sacred to Hinduism. The traditional themes of life and death are set forth and interwoven with many complex variations which give a kaleidoscopic picture of the development of almost three thousand years of Indian mythology.

SPEAKING OF ŚIVA

Translated by A. K. Ramanujan

Speaking of Śiva is a collection of *vacanas* or free-verse lyrics written by four major saints of the great *bhakti* protest movement which originated in the tenth century A.D.

Composed in Kannada, a Dravidian language of South India, the poems are lyrical expressions of love for the god Śiva. They mirror the urge to by-pass tradition and ritual, to concentrate on the subject rather than the object of worship, and to express kinship with all living things in moving terms. Passionate, personal, fiercely monotheistic, these free verses possess an appeal which is timeless and universal.

THE PENGUIN CLASSICS

THE KORAN

Translated by N. J. Dawood

The Koran 'is not only one of the greatest books of prophetic literature but also a literary masterpiece of surpassing excellence'. Unquestioningly accepted by Muslims to be the infallible word of Allah as revealed to Mohammed by the Angel Gabriel over thirteen hundred years ago, the Koran still provides the basic rules of conduct fundamental to the Arab way of life. Mr Dawood has produced a translation which retains the beauty of the original, altering the traditional arrangement to increase the understanding and pleasure for the uninitiated.

TALES FROM THE THOUSAND AND ONE NIGHTS

Translated by N. J. Dawood

Originating from India, Persia and Arabia, the *Tales from the Thousand and One Nights* represent the lively expression of a lay and secular imagination in revolt against religious austerity and zeal in Oriental literature. In this volume the translator has caught the freshness and spontaneity of the stories – which, although imaginative and extravagant, are a faithful mirror of medieval Islam.

BIRDS THROUGH A CEILING OF ALABASTER

THREE ABBASID POETS
ABBAS IBN AL-AHNAF, ABDULLAH IBN AL-MU'TAZZ,
ABU AL-ALA AL-MA'ARRI

Translated by Abdullah al-Udhari and George Wightman

Baghdad, throughout the Abbasid dynasty, was the centre of Arab–Muslim culture where the assimilation of Persian, Indian and Greek writing and thought produced a rich and diverse literature. The three poets represented in this volume wrote between the eighth and tenth centuries A.D., and range in mood from serious speculation to exuberant sensuality to delicate lyricism.

THE PENGUIN CLASSICS

THE BHAGAVAD GITA

Translated by Juan Mascaró

Sanskrit literature can boast some of the most beautiful and profoundly moving works of all times. It is essentially a romantic literature, interwoven with idealism and practical wisdom, expressing a passionate longing for spiritual vision. The eighteen chapters of the Bhagavad Gita (c. 500 B.C.) encompass the whole great struggle of a human soul. The three central themes of this immortal poem – Love, Light, and Life – arise from the symphonic vision of God in all things and of all things in God.

THE UPANISHADS

Translated and Selected by Juan Mascaró

The Upanishads represent for the Hindu approximately what the New Testament represents for the Christian. The earliest of these spiritual treatises, which vary greatly in length, were put down in Sanskrit between 800 and 400 B.C. This selection from twelve Upanishads reveals the paradoxical variety and unity, the great questions and simple answers, the spiritual wisdom and romantic imagination of these 'Himalayas of the Soul'.

THE DHAMMAPADA

Translated by Juan Mascaró

The Dhammapada is a collection of aphorisms which illustrate the Buddhist *dhamma* or moral system. Probably compiled in the third century B.C., the verses tell of the struggle towards Nirvana – the supreme goal for the Buddhist – and point out the narrow Path of Perfection which leads to it.

PELICAN BOOKS

BUDDHISM

Christmas Humphreys

Born in India in the sixth century B.C., Buddhism became the religion of Ceylon, Siam, Burma, and Cambodia, which adhere to the older or Southern School, while the developed Mahayana School is found in various forms in Tibet, Mongolia, China, Korea, and Japan.

To compress such a wealth of human thought into a single volume is difficult, but here is not only the history and development of Buddhism and the teaching of the various Schools, but also its condition in the world today.

THE BUDDHA

Trevor Ling

Professor Ling describes the origins of Buddhism, explaining the division into its principal variants, Mahayana and Theravada, and the continuity of Buddhist civilization in Ceylon after the resurgence of Hinduism on the mainland. At all times he sees the Buddhist *dhamma* as an entire way of life rather than a means of fulfilment, for the specifically religious aspect of Buddhist culture is but a small part of Siddhartha Gotama's world-embracing vision.

. . . and in the Penguin Classics

BUDDHIST SCRIPTURES

Translated by Edward Conze

Most of the writings chosen for this anthology were recorded between 100 and 400 A.D., the Golden Age of Buddhist literature. They include passages from the *Dharmapada*, the *Buddhacarita*, the *Questions of King Milinda*, and the *Tibetan Book of the Dead*. Dr Conze has concentrated on texts intended for the layman rather than for the monk and his selection exhibits more of the humanity than the profundity of the Scriptures. His translation shows a respect for the characteristic diction of Buddhist teachings and manages to preserve much of the original flavour.

THE PENGUIN CLASSICS

Some Recent and Forthcoming Volumes

THE PSALMS

Translated by Peter Levi

BALZAC

SELECTED SHORT STORIES

Translated by Sylvia Raphael

FLAUBERT

SALAMMBO

Translated by A. J. Krailsheimer

ZOLA

LA BÊTE HUMAINE

Translated by Leonard Tancock

A NIETZSCHE READER

Translated by R. J. Hollingdale

CAO XUEQIN

THE STORY OF THE STONE VOLUME TWO:

THE CRAB-FLOWER CLUB

Translated by David Hawkes

BALZAC

THE WILD ASS'S SKIN

Translated by H. J. Hunt

CICERO

LETTERS TO ATTICUS

Translated by D. R. Shackleton Bailey